Home

Chicana & Chicano Visions of the Américas

CHICANA & CHICANO VISIONS OF THE AMÉRICAS

Series Editor

Robert Con Davis-Undiano

Editorial Board

Rudolfo Anaya

Denise Chávez

David Draper Clark

María Amparo Escandón

María Herrera-Sobek

Rolando Hinojosa-Smith

Demetria Martínez

Carlos Monsiváis

Rafael Pérez-Torres

Leroy V. Quintana

José David Saldívar

Ramón Saldívar

Randy Lopez Goes Home

A Novel

Rudolfo Anaya

UNIVERSITY OF OKLAHOMA PRESS : NORMAN

This is a work of fiction. Names, characters, places, and incidents are either the product of the author's imagination or are used fictitiously, and any resemblance to actual events, locales, or persons, living or dead, is entirely coincidental.

Library of Congress Cataloging-in-Publication Data

Anaya, Rudolfo A.
Randy Lopez goes home: a novel / Rudolfo Anaya.
    p.   cm.— (Chicana & Chicano visions of the Américas)
ISBN 978-0-8061-4189-3 (cloth)
ISBN 978-0-8061-4457-3 (paper)
1. Mexican Americans—Fiction.
2. Spiritual life—Fiction.
3. New Mexico—Fiction.
I. Title.
PS3551.N27R36 2011
813'.54—dc22
                                              2010051723

Randy Lopez Goes Home: A Novel is Volume 9 in the Chicana & Chicano Visions of the Américas series.

The paper in this book meets the guidelines for permanence and durability of the Committee on Production Guidelines for Book Longevity of the Council on Library Resources, Inc. ∞

    4 5 6 7 8 9 10

For Patricia, mi querida
esposa y compañera

Randy Lopez Goes Home

One

Randy arrives in Agua Bendita, where time stands still.

Randy Lopez rode a sway-back mare into the village of Agua Bendita. The small hamlet sat astride a bucolic river wrapped in a time that seemed to have no time. Village clocks had stopped long ago. Only the river continued to run. Over the centuries the relentless water had cut a narrow valley through the piedmont.

The old people of the valley used to say the river, with its nurturing water, was one of the four sacred rivers torn loose from Eden.

Night and day the river sang its song, a song that changed with the seasons. The mist of ancient legends swirled all around; music echoed along the dark canyon.

Agua Bendita sat at the foot of a dormant volcano. The mountain appeared quiet, but beneath the trembling earth in measureless caverns boiled lakes of hot magma, like those in Dante's *Inferno*.

The magma heated veins of water that bubbled to the surface through cracks in the crust. Hot springs dotted the valley. In times past people had bathed in the springs.

Many claimed they had been cured from diseases after bathing in the miraculous waters. Perhaps that's why the hispanos who had settled in the ancient valley called their village Agua Bendita.

The villagers heard noises, but no one knew where they

came from. Some said they were the agony of lost spirits who wandered along the river.

Randy whispered, Whoa. The tired mare stopped, shifted under his weight, and breathed a sigh of relief. She dropped last night's meager meal, compost the rains would wash down to the river. Food for the fish, fish for the fishermen.

The sullen sun cast no shadows. The slate sky hung immobile.

That's strange, Randy thought. This morning on my way to Santa Fe the sun was shining.

Oso, Randy's trusty dachshund, barked. The small dog looked around as if to say what in the hell are we doing here? Let's go home.

Randy shivered. We are home, he assured his dog.

A big, hairy tarantula lumbered across the road. That's why Randy had stopped. He didn't want to hurt the huge spider. Was it going to weave a web like Arachne of old? Or was this Spider Woman of native lore?

No way to know.

Why was it crossing the road? Time on the other side was the same as time on this side. Or was it?

Was the tarantula answering a territorial instinct? Did it cross to deposit its progeny on the earth of its birth? So many of nature's creatures returned to their ancestral homes when their time came to an end.

Was it a law of nature to go from there to here?

A gob of chewing tobacco splashed near the spider, and it moved forward a few inches.

Two old cowboys standing on the porch of La Cantina laughed. They were taking turns spitting tobacco juice—not to hit the spider, but to urge it to move on.

Randy took out his tattered notebook and made a note: Humans, like spiders, cross roads when gobs hit nearby. Gobs of ambition, greed, love, lust, grief, war, or family. Or just blind inertia resting in every man's soul. Nonsense.

Randy had attended night school. He had written a book: *My Life Among the Gringos*. One note read: Gringos move a lot. From east to west. To the sea. To the moon. What drives them? Manifest destiny as construed from Darwin's opus?

The Anglos, those whom Randy called gringos, took readily to the white man's burden.

I'm home, Randy whispered. What drove me here?

Home was Agua Bendita, one of the hispano villages in northern New Mexico that dotted the mountain. The Lopez family had settled here generations ago. A mostly traditional, Spanish-speaking family.

But times had changed, and it became difficult for a young man to make a living in the mountains. So Randy had set out to make his fortune, and that meant he had to learn the gringo way of life. They ran the world, it seemed.

Randy had written: They love to run things, to organize. Been doing it a long time. Still are.

He looked down the road, but he couldn't remember where his father's house stood. A pomegranate tree used to grow in the front yard. He would look for that.

Across the river lived the illusive Sofia. She had haunted Randy's dreams since childhood. Legend told that three times she had lost her virginity.

What did it mean?

A cherry tree grew in her father's orchard. Randy remembered boys swimming across the river to pillage the ripe, juicy cherries. Or did they go to catch a glimpse of Sofia?

Wisdom is to be cultivated, Randy's father had taught him. Be wise. Ten juicio. Wisdom was a cultural value.

So Randy fell in love with Sofia. As a child he sat on the bank of the river and dreamed of Sofia. He read all the books his teacher would let him take home from school.

Someday I will know Sofia, he promised himself. But first he had to explore the world beyond Agua Bendita.

In those days that meant to go and live among the gringos. In many ways it still does.

Go and learn all you can, Sofia said. I'll wait for you under the cherry tree.

Perhaps it was that pledge that drove Randy out of the village and into the world.

Another gob of tobacco juice splattered, and again the tarantula moved a few inches, its dim brain telling it that it didn't want to be burned by tobacco spittle. Life is like that. We don't want to get burned.

Randy thought of the cherry tree in Sofia's yard. The tree would be bare now, its ripe cherries picked long ago.

Today was Día de los Muertos. A cold breeze blew down the canyon. Tree branches rattled. Again he heard a distinctive guitar-and-fiddle melody.

He shivered.

Had he forgotten Sofia? Did he return to Agua Bendita seeking her or something else? What discomfort stirred his soul? Was he afraid that he had lost his identity in the land of the gringos? To thine own self be true, his father had said often. Tú eres tú. Be proud. No manches la bandera. Don't stain our flag, our family honor.

Had he changed by leaving the ways of his ancestors?

Dimé con quién andas y te diré quién eres. An old dicho. Tell me who your friends are, and I'll tell you who you are. Very true. The pack made the wolf.

The two cowboys on the porch of the cantina were not real

cowboys. Not in the true sense. Someone had told Randy that all the Old West cowboys were dead. The West was dying. Or dead. The two old men were playing cowboy. Torn jeans and scruffy boots. Greasy baseball gimme caps. Just two old men who had nothing to do but hang around the cantina. Bothersome souls.

Where you going cowboy? one asked.

Here, Randy replied.

What for?

I was born in Agua Bendita.

The two laughed.

You been on the road too long, Pancho.

Once in a while a prejudiced person called a Mexican Pancho. Randy had written that in his book.

Why? he asked.

Cause they changed the name to Hot Springs, thas why. Try an get newcomers to take the hot baths. That old Aqua Vendida name don cut it.

Hot Springs? Had he come up the wrong road? The place looked familiar, but . . .

I used to live here.

Use to don mean squat, one said. Come on in n have a beer, whoever you are.

Randy. My name's Randy Lopez.

Come on in, Randy.

Thank you, but I have to water the mare.

Down the road. One pointed, and they went back to spitting tobacco juice.

Americanos. They could be a welcoming kind, open-hearted, willing to help a stranger. But his godfather didn't like the americanos. Over and over he told Randy how they had stolen the hispano land grants. His constant lament.

His godfather called the americanos gringos. Maybe that's where Randy had learned the word.

Randy had read history. He could make generalizations, but he knew that labels often didn't get at the truth. The gringos, like most other clans, could be illusive.

One final gob of chewing tobacco hit the tarantula squarely on its back. It squirmed. It would not pass on its genes. It would not make it across the road.

Two

The old cowboy explains bet-him-Mike's-horses, or becoming bear scat.

Randy moved on. He needed to water the mare and feed Oso. He spotted an old man brushing a gelding.

I need water, Randy called.

Hep yuself, the man replied.

Randy led the mare into the corral, threw some hay, and fed Oso a few stale potato chips he found in his pocket.

Buenos días, señor. How much for the hay?

The old man laughed. No need for money here.

That's a fine-looking Appaloosa.

Espíritu Santo. Spirit for short. Bought him from natives up in Wyoming, oh maybe twenty years ago. We seen our better days.

Wyoming?

Yup. I cowboyed there when I was young. Came down here n built a house for my wife. Me? I never could sleep on a mattress.

You still ranch? Randy asked a stupid question. He knew better.

Cowboying is dead. Too dang bad.

Randy nodded. He had heard.

The Old West is dead. Like my friend Max said, it turned into a Hollywood movie set. They made movies that was just plain dumb. Then we went to the movies to see how we lived. We're in a movie right now n those dumb jokers don get it. Best to leave.

He wiped his sweaty brow and asked, You from around here?

I was born here—

Sooner or later we come home, the old man said before Randy could finish.

You leaving?

Yup. I tried a nursin home. The food kilt me. Get old n thas all you get. A nursin home. A man caint rightly go in a bed-pan.

Randy smiled. He guessed the old man would know.

I'm gonna ride up the mountain. Bear country. Spirit here'll come back. Me? The bears'll eat me. Become bear scat. Thas all.

Randy waited.

We die n become something else. The sway-back— whose?

I was on foot. I guess on my way here. A man at the entrance of the canyon took pity and said I could use her.

Did he have a stuffed two-headed calf by the door?

Yes, Randy replied.

That be Todos Santos. He tole everyone the calf was born under some special zodiac sign. Maybe like the Indians' white buffalo. The calf lived a year or so, then died. Same zodiac sign. A complete season. Todos Santos was heart-broke. So he figured a way to stuff the dead animal. Bay leaves, I think. Every soul that passes to here has to see that calf.

It scared the hell out of me, Randy said.

The old man laughed. Good. You passed the test. Thas why Todos Santos lent you the mare.

Told me to turn her loose and she'll go back.

They trot home. Unlike women.

Randy thought best not to comment about women.

What else he say to you?

He said not to look back.

Did you?

No, sir.

Smart boy. You look back n you lose your way. Some say you turn into a pillar of salt. Like Lot's wife. I think you just become a lost soul. Wandering forever. Better *here*.

Randy agreed even though he didn't know what the man meant by *here*.

The old man led the Appaloosa into the corral, where it rubbed noses with the mare. Then he sat under the dry branches of the ramada to smoke. He motioned for Randy to sit.

A horse is smarter than a man, he said. That mare was a beautiful woman in another life. Her husband abused her, so the sway back.

You believe in—

Yup. We jus go on becomin somethin else. Bet-him-Mike's-horses. A Greek word. But that knowledge is old as the Hindus. Means the flesh dies but the soul moves to a new home. Thas all.

Bet-him-Mike's-horses. Randy rolled the word silently on his tongue. The soul moves on. Did he mean met-emp-sy-chosis? Yes. The old man was describing transmigration of the soul.

I like that, Randy said. Bet-him-Mike's-horses.

I don't know Greek, but it's clear. One dies and the soul finds a new body. So they say.

Randy thought of Tibet and the Dalai Lama.

Ideas like that had become popular in the sixties. During the hippie era a few gringo kids had gotten into Zen Buddhism. Not too many. Their parents wanted them to be doctors or attorneys. Make money.

The flower children had created a culture of love and peace. Flower power. The summer of Woodstock. For a while there was hope in gringolandia. The hippies broke down old rules. Then they got to middle age and made new rules.

Cycles.

The old man pursed his lips. Your dog there was a German prince left over from the old Hapsburgs. You can tell by its curly hair. I figure a person got to be a kind human to be reborn a horse or a dog. They're on a higher plane. Thas all.

He looked at Randy. You, son. You thought of how nature recycles?

Not much, Randy said.

I see. Plenty of time here. You was born here?

Yes.

Baptized?

In the river.

The old man nodded. The song of the river's in you. Listen.

They listened. Faint music blended with spirit songs that cascaded down the side of the canyon.

Randy's father had told him that long ago the original natives lived on the cliffs. Truth was they lived all over the northern mountains, all over the country, before they were displaced. Sooner or later everyone was displaced.

At night I hear a woman singing at the river.

La Llorona? Randy asked.

The old man smiled. Not the Crying Woman. She only cries when she chases Mexican kids.

Maybe a mermaid, Randy suggested.

Like those Ulysseus met on his journey? No, truth is it's my wife. She died a year back. Now it's just me n Spirit here.

Life can be lonely—

The dead should move on. She should'uv become a seal in

Inuit waters. Or a beautiful bird in a Costa Rica rain forest. No, she stayed here n sings at night.

The people used to say they heard noises.

Yup. Bothersome.

I see, Randy said, though he didn't.

The dead should pick a place they once knew n loved. Where they can maybe see old friends. A place they can be fulfilled. He paused. But we do not tell the powerful forces of the universe where we wanna go.

What about heaven?

The old man smiled. I see Christianity took on you. Thas fine. Me, I'll take my chances with the bears n coyotes. Speaking of coyotes, you gotta watch your dog.

We ran into four coyotes when we crossed la Cañada de Juan Diego, but they didn't bother Oso.

He's a ghost dog, thas why. Good. He be safe from the critters. They gotta eat too, you know.

He flipped the cigarette butt, went to his horse, put a halter on the gelding, and threw an old sarape over its back.

We're ready, he whispered. He led the horse to an old tree stump and mounted.

I'll help, Randy said, jumping up.

Don need hep anymore. I worked hard all my life. This is the last time I mount. Goin up there. He nodded toward the green peaks of the mountain. Spirit will come home. Will you brush him down n throw some hay?

Yes, sir. I will.

In the end it's bear n coyote scat. Much better for nature than bein stuck in a box in the ground.

He started off, then stopped.

By the way, what was your father's name?

Juan Diego Lopez.

Those that settled the old land grant?

Yes, sir.

I see. Mexicans been in these mountains since Oñate. Damn near four hundred years. You got the mountain in your blood. Your mother was an Indian from the pueblo. Beautiful woman. Juan Diego got her cause he had blue eyes. The man could ride. One Día de San Juan he pulled all the roosters from the ground. You got good blood.

Thank you.

You can sleep in the shed. If there be sleep to be had. Keep the mare in the corral long as you want. The house up on the hill— I built it for my wife. Locked up now. Nothin lasts on this earth.

Randy nodded. Once upon a wistful time, he had heard his father sigh and say, Todo se acaba.

The old man touched the sides of the Appaloosa and started up-river. Randy watched. A gray mist seemed to rise even though it was almost midday. After a while he could not see the horse or the man.

The sun was setting on the Western Isles. A season had ended. The empire was sinking.

The old man would ride up into ponderosa country. Among the towering trees he would find one particular old pine tree, dismount, take the halter off the horse, and tell it to trot home.

He would cover himself with the sarape and wait. The animals would come. After a few days crows would pick out his eyes. Coyotes would rip at him, then later the bears. The old man would smile as he moved into some new form.

Randy looked around. Maybe it wasn't the West that was dead. Maybe he was just dreaming.

Three

Those reincarnation guys have it made … they just keep on being recycled.

Randy sighed. It was good to be back home. But why was he feeling so nostalgic? Was it because the old man had gone to become bear scat? Wasn't there something poetic in his choice? In his courage?

There was hope in the old man's heart. He would become something new. A new form. Did form imply ideal? The soul? Ah, well.

Those reincarnation guys have it made, thought Randy. They never die, they just keep on being recycled. Eternal bliss waits at the end. Nirvana. Most religions promise some kind of heaven. That, or hell.

Follow your bliss, the poet had said. What did he mean?

It didn't matter what side of the coin you landed on, both were equally complicated.

Someone behind him shouted, !Oye! !Ven ayúdame!

Randy jumped. A priest appeared from nowhere. His large head was twisted into his shrunken right shoulder.

Me? Randy asked.

!Sí, tú! ?Que 'stás sordo?

No—

!Ven acá! !Ándale! !Apúrate!

Randy followed the stocky, bow-legged cura to the river, where a huge cross lay half-submerged in the water.

!Levántala! the priest pointed.

Lift the cross?

¡Sí! Lift the cross! ¡Ay Dios, dame paciencia!

Randy cringed. What the hell was going on?

Me?

¡Sí, pendejo, *me!* ?Qué no hablas español, la lengua de tus padres? Do you speak English?

Sí, I mean yes. I learned in the land of the gringos—

Gringos? Shhh. We don't call them that anymore. Say Anglos.

Randy nodded. Of course he knew most people referred to the gringos as Anglos. He knew the history of the Anglo Saxons. They ruled England long ago. Queen Elizabeth sent the royal navy and some of her pirates around the world. The English language spread. And their genes. Their race increased.

In years past their language had arrived in Agua Bendita, initiating a difficult time of transition for the Spanish-speaking hispanos.

I speak English, Randy protested. I read Shakespeare, the Bible, *Harry Potter*—

An educated pendejo! the priest scowled. How nice. So you know it's more polite to call them Anglos.

Even if they're not, Randy thought. Not all whites liked to be called Anglos. The Irish and German Americans aren't Anglos. Labeling people was a tricky business. Will I have to change the title of my book? *My Life Among the Anglos*. That doesn't have a ring to it. People might think it's a travel book.

Anda, pick up the cross.

That's a big cross, thought Randy. Made of mountain fir, probably by a Taos santero. Must weigh a ton. Twelve feet long, one foot for each of the apostles. Perhaps that's why the priest's shoulder is shrunken.

Where to? he asked.

To the church. It's been here since Día de San Juan, when I blessed the water. Now pick it up! A little penance will do you good.

Randy shook his head. I don't know if I can—

Yes, you can! You're young! And I can't wait! Mass at noon. The penitentes disappeared! Went to the fiesta. ¡Cabrones! This should be their penance! But oh no, they only do their thing on Good Friday. The rest of the year I bear the cross!

There's a fiesta?

Sí, tonto. Can't you hear the music?

What's the celebration?

Día de los Muertos. Day of the Dead. Where have you been? The Matachines from Bernalillo are dancing. Old timers. Most can't remember the steps. There's a corrida de gallo. Pulling the buried roosters from the ground. By midnight they'll all be drunk. ¡Qué vergüenza!

He turned his large owl-eyes on Randy. I know who you are!

Who?

You're one of Levi Rael's boys! The converso! Old Levi pretended he was a good Catholic, prayed the Lord's Prayer louder than anyone, but he was still a Jew. They came with Oñate. Claimed to be católicos, but they secretly pray on Fridays. He made the sign of the cross.

No, Randy protested.

Oh yes, you are! That's why you can't pick up the cross!

I can!

Randy entered the cold water, struggled, and finally lifted the cross over his right shoulder.

Good boy! the priest clapped.

Randy grunted. He felt his spine crack, his shoulder buckle.

To the church?

¡Sí! ¡Vamos!

Oso bared his teeth. Gerrrrr, growling in English.

¡Pinche perro! The priest kicked at Oso.

Randy looked at the church sitting at the top of the hill like a tired old maid. He would never make it. Still, to prove he was not a converso, to show he really was a good Catholic, he would tote the load.

¡Con ganas! the priest cried, and Randy strained forward, farted.

The bank was steep. He dug his boots into the clay and heaved. He stumbled, nearly fell. Sweat broke out, his nose bled, his eyes bulged. Why me? he wondered.

¡Ándale! the priest called. ¡Dale gas!

It took nearly an hour to reach the church. The priest opened the door and Randy struggled down the aisle.

On the side walls, someone from long ago had painted the Stations of the Cross. Jesus carrying the cross on the road to Calvary.

I prayed here as a boy, Randy remembered. Sunday mass and every Friday during Lent. But praying was not like carrying the cross. Prayer is easy; the cross weighs a ton.

Reality is always more difficult.

There! The priest pointed to a hole by the side of the altar. In the pozo! ¡Ándale!

Using all the strength he had left, Randy reached the altar. He placed the foot of the cross by the hole, lifted, and the cross slid in. Breathing a sigh of relief, he crumpled to the floor.

Muy bien, the priest smiled. You get an indulgence. One hour free from the fires of hell. But that's all. And tell your converso brothers I better see them in church.

My father, Randy panted, was Juan Diego Lopez de la Cañada de Juan del Oso. He was católico.

The priest looked closely at Randy. So you're not one of Levi Rael's boys?

No.

You look like Levi. Did you change your name?

I was named for three saints, but at school the teacher called me Randy. It stuck.

I know that bruja. She's Presbyterian! Went around changing the names of our niños. Now all the kids have gringo— I mean Anglo names. What can we do, we live in the time of the gringo.

I wrote that in my book, Randy whispered, massaging his bruised shoulder.

Maybe the teacher did you a favor. By naming you Randy, you could fit into their society. Today only the mexicano immigrants use the saints' names. José María, Ángel, Guadalupe. It drives Motor Vehicles crazy. Why are men given female names? they ask. ¡Pendejos! Don't they know the holy names?

I made my first communion here.

The priest studied Randy. I don't remember you.

I attended the Stations of the Cross during Lent. I sat there with my family.

Juan Diego Lopez, the priest pondered.

Yes. Do you remember him?

No. I don't. Time is like a worm. It eats everything.

Even memory?

Yes. Even memory.

Four

Randy meets Lilith, who washes his hands and anoints him.

Bent and bruised from the weight of the cross, Randy hobbled down the road. Oso trailed behind, sniffing the stalks of withered wildflowers and giving chase to frivolous magpies. The birds squawked, limped a few feet, then flew off when Oso gave chase. All enjoyed the game.

In the distance Randy heard the sound of drumming. The fiesta. Perhaps there he could find someone who remembered him.

!Por Dios! a woman called. ?Qué te pasó? Did you fall? Are you hurt?

Randy turned to face a short, full-breasted woman. Her round face held the age-old beauty of the millennium. A real Venus, Randy thought. She carried a sack of potatoes. There was no meat in Agua Bendita.

Randy explained what had happened.

Father Polonio made you carry the cross? He should be ashamed! He saw you were newly arrived and made you do his daily penance. I hope he doesn't make a habit of it.

Randy agreed.

Pobre padre. He still hasn't made his peace with the conversos. It takes all kinds I say; why impose? Your hands are bleeding. Come with me. She pointed. I live right here.

Can I help?

We're beyond help.

My dog?

He can come. I see he is constant. I have a biscuit for him. She opened the door and laid the sack down. Randy and Oso followed her in.

The simple abode reminded Randy of his parents' home. Hand-carved wood furniture. The doily on a chair reminded him of the doily that once covered his father's chair. His mother would always remove it when his father sat in his chair in the evening.

Nostalgic fragments kept washing over him. Pleasant sensations.

The woman's house was cold. A breeze moved the curtains.

My name is Lilith. But I have had many names. Isis, Astarte, Venus, Ishtar, Devi, Aditi, never Virgin. She laughed. But why bother you with that? Sit here.

I'm Randy. He sat and she brought a basin of water, soap, and a towel. Tenderly she washed his hands.

Like large, fully ripe pears, her breasts swayed beneath her blouse of quilted feathers. Randy looked away.

There, she said. My soap will heal those cuts. Her face glowed like a full moon on a starless night. She was lovely.

Your shoulder. Take off your shirt.

He removed his jacket and shirt and she rubbed a fragrant oil on his bruised shoulder. Coconut oil? Or almond? Where in the hell did she get such oils in Agua Bendita?

Could this be the land of miracles? Or was she a witch? It didn't matter. The pain seeped away.

Thank you.

De nada.

He put on his shirt and jacket.

You speak Spanish.

I thought you knew?

What?

21

Once, I spoke Sumerian, Aramaic, Urdu. There are many languages *here*. The river, the birds, the wind always moaning, the trees singing, the spirits complaining. So many voices.

I see. You live alone?

I was destined to give birth to many generations. Wide hips. She smiled and swayed. And other attributes, she added with a wink.

She's clearly proud of her stature, Randy surmised. A robust woman whose body is testament to many births.

My husbands all went in search of some golden fleece or other, as many men do. So what? I stayed and populated the world. I was no whore, mind you. Just fertile.

Randy nodded. Thank you, he said again.

I think Father Polonio is crazy. Why make you carry the cross? It's he who needs the penance. Too much religion in the world if you ask me. Each one wants to be the voice of god. God is here. In the belly, where lies fertility. She touched her rotund stomach. Why can't we all agree?

There is power in religion and in governments, Randy said. Once they have it, they don't give it up.

Yes. And that's why so many parts of the world have gone up in flames. The fire of god is raging throughout. At first I thought it was the apocalypse, but no. Each person could have prevented the chaos. They blamed it on the Maya calendar. !Pendejos! The year 2012 was for the Maya people, not for every tonto who comes along. People should have helped mother nature, our earth. But they didn't.

Yes. I agree.

At least here we are safe, she said with some finality.

How do you mean? Randy asked.

Peace. Everyone wants to rest in peace. Is that why you came?

I was born here.

Ah! she cried and smiled. I sense you have the blood of the river and the mountain. Where have you been?

I went to work in the city. Fast-food places, construction, you name it. Then I joined the navy. There I learned about the world, and the—

The Others, she said.

Randy nodded, not knowing quite what she meant.

Tell me. I hear so little.

The navy sent me to Fort Bliss.

That's in the desert!

Yes. I guess my life has been like that. It was okay.

How?

I bought a pair of scissors in Juárez. Started giving the soldiers haircuts on weekends. I got pretty good at it. When I got out I cut hair for friends. Once a friend of a friend asked me to cut his hair. He was ready to invest some money, but didn't know how to proceed. I told him I was sure he would do the right thing. He made a fortune. He said it was because of my advice. He told others and they came seeking advice. I told each one I knew he would do the right thing.

Brilliant! Lilith exclaimed. You have a gift.

I don't think so. I did learn that people are greedy. The more they get the more they want.

A vice that has caused so much ruin, she agreed. El que mucho traga se ahoga. Those whose only goal is to make money drown in their greed. And they pull others into the vortex. Where there is greed, there will be tragedy.

I got other jobs. Once I worked in a bookstore. I could read all the books. But everything was changing. Electronic books. The world became virtual. People became disoriented. They didn't know if they were in reality or virtual reality. I left.

But I sense another reason.

I grew lonely.

Ah, the common ailment of man. We wonder why god gave us hearts. They are broken so often.

I had a vision of love. Sofia. We were sweethearts, well, almost. It was here I first caught a glimpse of her.

Sofia who thrice lost her virginity? We call her Sofia of the Lambs. She raises sheep for wool. She lives alone.

Where?

Across the river.

That's her! I must go.

Wait! There's no bridge. The armies of good and evil fought a war. The bridge was destroyed.

I'll find a way—

She touched his hand. Did you really come looking for Sofia? Or is it yourself you seek?

You're right. I feel I lost part of my soul. But I have carried Sofia in my heart all these years.

Then you are a Lover in search of the Beloved. But what if Sofia is a dream, an illusion? The world is full of illusions.

Randy sighed. Lilith spoke the truth. He wondered if Sofia were only a dream. So many images appeared in the web of his dreams, like shadows cast against a wall.

Had he been fooling himself all these years? Sofia might not recognize him.

He squared his shoulders. I'll go to her, and she must tell me if I'm dreaming.

That's the spunk! Lilith said. But how? An avenging angel came with a flaming sword and struck the bridge into splinters.

I thought you said it was destroyed during the war between good and evil.

There are many versions. Pick the one you like. The world has always been divided, so why should it be different here? Anyway, no one can cross to the other side until a new bridge is built. Over there is another world. You do understand that many worlds exist?

Yes. Randy knew about the many worlds. The world of the child dissolved into that of the teenager, then the man, work, marriage, children, and finally old age. Everyone crossed from one world to the next on a bridge, and when one crossed, the world left behind seemed to disappear. The bridge dissolved.

Only memories were left of those prior times. And memories, too, evaporated.

I am young. I can build a bridge.

It can be dangerous, she warned. Sofia's world is one of hard-earned wisdom. We catch images of Sofia in dreams. Perhaps she is the illusive Anima. The Beloved we seek in the dream-world.

The Anima *is* the Beloved. I like that, Randy said. Such a woman visits me in my dreams. She is a shadow. A guide. I thought it was Sofia.

Dream images teach us the wisdom of the ages. They are as close as we get to heaven.

Is Sofia such a shadow? he asked.

Wisdom and Anima are sisters. When they awaken in the soul, a person acquires great power. Love flourishes.

Then I must go to her. I do love her.

Good! Lilith exclaimed. Every man needs a purpose! Even a deceptive one. That's why men stumble through life. We are caught in a karmic wheel, as some say. But what the hell. I'll help you.

You will?

Yes. You need to cut trees for the bridge. I can bring potatoes from my garden for you to eat.

I don't know how to thank you.

She hugged him and swarms of golden honeybees dripping sweet honey flew from the honeycombs between her breasts. Sticky as woman's ovum, aromatic as a field of purple-flowering clover.

Randy felt comforted. You are as warm and caring as my mother.

Every woman is mother to men, she said. Despot or saint, they are all the fruit of our Life Force.

Randy felt dumb. Woman *was* the Life Force. He should have known. His mother. Sofia. It began to make sense.

Look. Your dog has eaten the biscuit. Come. I bake the most divine potato pancakes. And my potato soup has won prizes. On a full stomach you can continue. One does not have to starve to see the face of God. One sees more clearly with a full stomach. Ask those who suffer from hunger.

Five

Bob and Squat take Randy into La Cantina, where violent spirits abide. Randy meets Abel's Daughter.

Lilith's garden looked worn and gray. The corn plants from another century were now dry and withered. The pollen, if there had been pollen, was now dry dust on the tassels.

In the old days the natives from the pueblo had gathered the sacred pollen. Did they still? Or had everything changed?

Vague empty shells of tomatoes, cucumbers, melons, and pumpkins lay scattered among the tangled vines.

Great horned owls sat in the trees, observing the desolation.

The valley looks different, Randy said. Things look old.

Not much to do here, Lilith replied. In the mornings I deliver potatoes. In the afternoons I read. Nights are eternal.

Eternal?

Yes.

Amaranth. Amaryllis. Tulips. Dank and dead. Rows of yellowed hollyhocks crumbling in the breeze.

The hollyhock is the flower of Agua Bendita, she explained. They were brought to us by San José, the stepfather of Jesus. Legend tells us he visited Agua Bendita. He stuck his staff in the ground and it blossomed into a hollyhock. The wind spread the dark seeds. But legends are a dime a dozen here. Many think our flower should be the marigold. Flower of the dead. But the old-timers were fond of las Varas de San José.

Traditions, Randy said.

Yes.

I should go.

Stay loyal to Sofia no matter what.

I will.

He thanked Lilith, and went to check on the mare. She had water and hay. He brushed her down, then went down the road followed by Oso.

How does one build a bridge? he was wondering when the two old codgers standing on the cantina's porch called to him.

Hey Pancho, come in n cool off. The beer's warm n stinks to high heaven. They laughed and punched each other.

Do you know anything about building bridges? Randy asked.

Shoot, yeah. We can build mansions in the sky! Liar, liar, pants on fire! They laughed again.

Randy followed them into the dark cantina. Spectral figures sat at the tables. Pain was evident on their contorted faces. All were armed with pistols, rifles, and other deadly weapons.

By the way, my name's Squat. This here's Bob. Bob and Squat!

Is it safe? Randy asked.

Don mind them, Squat replied. They're ordinry citizens. Thas how they chose to get here.

Their choice? Randy asked.

Yup. It's in the Constitution. Oh, there are accidents. But forget that. People kill people, not guns. Let's have a beer.

Waitress! Bob called. Bring us them twenty-nine bottles of beer on the wall! We'll take one down n pass it around.

A young woman approached and served them beers.

This here's Abel's Daughter, Bob said.

Abel? I knew Abel, Randy said, looking into the face of the girl. He coached our baseball team. Lived across the Arroyo de Doña Sebastiana. Dogtown we called it.

***

Yes. She smiled.

You were just a baby. He carried you on his shoulders.

There was a car wreck, Abel's Daughter said. We were on our way to a wedding in Chimayó. A drunk driver ran into us. A terrible explosion. Everyone was thrown out of the car.

A horrible fate, Squat whispered as Abel's Daughter walked away.

A lovely girl, Randy said.

Whas your name?

Randy. I was born here—

Really? When?

On the Fourth of July.

Fourth of July? Damn! Why din they name you Liberty, or Justice, or Don Tread on Me?

My padrinos gave me the name of three saints—

Pad-reenos, shoot! Three saints don mean squat here. Bob spat on the floor. The DMZ has reached Santa Fe. Messicans coming to el norte, so they call it. Babies born here git to be American citizens! Aint right!

It's in the Constitution, Bob.

Bullshit! I don believe the Constitution!

Randy had seen the weary lines of mexicanos trudging north. The economies of war, greed, and a country hooked on drugs had created a diaspora.

Each brown-skinned man walked with the tools of his trade slung over his shoulder. Wives walked beside their husbands, guarding their children like mother hens.

Venimos a trabajar, y no pedimos limosna, they sang. We come to work, we do not beg. A new corrido was being born. A ballad the tired immigrants sang in their camps at night.

Randy thought of Woody Guthrie's ballads for the workers from another time. Later, the corridos for César Chávez.

Things didn't change much.

They're on Welfare! Bob continued his harangue. They speak Spanish! There goes our way of life! They take our jobs!

Hell, Bob, you haven't worked in years! Squat said. Bent over in the fields, short hoes, construction or tarring roofs— thas wicked labor. Only pintos and Messicans do it.

Oh yeah? Bob got in Randy's face. You wanna build a bridge? Maybe those Messicans will help you. They're your people, aint they?

They're your people. A phrase used by the demagogues on television to create divisions among people. And by politicians who for their own gain created animosity among groups.

Your people means us, thought Randy. They know *us* as the *Others*. Every group blames the Others when things go wrong.

My parents taught me to respect everyone, but was I respected? Did I create my own Others? I wrote about my life among the gringos to expose prejudice, not because I hate anyone. I learned about us and they. My country right or wrong. Love it or leave it. Now those in power want the Mexicans to leave. Who was next? Some things had changed, but the three-headed dragon continued to spew its poison. Racism. Ignorance. Fear.

Things're gettin better, Squat said.

Randy made a note: Try telling that to the poor.

Randy tasted the beer. Fermented potatoes. The spirit in the bottle was bitter. Really angry at something or someone. He pushed the bottle away.

Where the bridge to? Bob slobbered.

Across the river.

Squat grabbed Randy's arm. Oh 'migo, you don wanna go there. They say thas the land of dead Aztecs n old desert prophets. Their bones rattle at night. The babes of limbo cry constantly. All the innocents of war, those disappeared by dictators, victims of the Holocaust. . . . He went on and on.

His friend Bob interrupted. Squat! You don know squat! Aint no dead Aztecs out there! Just dead poets.

Dead poets?

Yeah.

Poets don hurt no one. We caint cross cause it's the River of the Dead. The Geeks called it the River Sticks. Need a guide to get across.

A guide?

Yeah. Like a wise old cure-in-dera or somethin.

Love is my guide, Randy said.

Love! The two men laughed and punched each other.

Lilith told me Sofia of the Lambs lives there.

Lilith is a witch! Squat exclaimed. Claims she can grow corn. Bullshit!

Bob slurped his beer. With that body she can grow *anythin!* he laughed.

Hol on, Bob. Mabbe she can. We don judge a person's gifts anymore. We're pas judgin the livin n the dead. Give the kid a chance. Go on, Randy. Tell us.

Maybe there is some hope in paradise, Randy suggested.

Hope? Not likely. The old Hispanics said a few saints live there. And used-up angels. Like a retiremen home for those dat lost their wings. Least, thas the legend I heard.

Gawd Awlmighty, this place is full of legends! Stories. Fantasy. You caint believe a thing!

But it's all we got.

That n this beer. Yuk.

Bob leaned into Randy. Is this Sofia worth it?

Randy nodded. I carried her in my heart all this time. There was so little meaning left in the world; she was all he had to hold on to.

Believe in booze, Squat suggested. Drugs, legal or not, prescriptions, home-cooked meth, anythin dat makes reality n its pain disappear. Thas how lotsa *these* folks got here.

The world is cookin hot stuff. Smoke, snort, or cut a vein.

All ideals have died, so why hurry?

Get rich, be happy.

Sorry, we caint hep you.

Stay here, Squat suggested. Abel's Daughter's alone and lonely. She's younger'n you, but what the hell, a pound of flesh is a pound of flesh.

She is lovely, Randy said, but his love was for Sofia.

A haggard woman nearby coughed and swore. Gonna kill ebery las gawd dem un-unmerican . . . bastar—

Squat shouted at her. There aint no god to swear at, so shut up!

Randy looked around. Those at the tables were staring at him with vacant eyes. They had heard. The young man wanted to build a bridge across the river. Soon the rumor would spread.

But why? they whispered. It's quiet *here*. Or at least it's all we got.

Está loco, an old man whispered.

Even the Indians from the pueblo who still prayed and danced for rain said, Está loco.

The gringos in the cantina agreed. A Mexican boy could never build a bridge. Hadn't he failed high school? Didn't get his diploma. Still had a noticeable accent when he spoke English. Would never get ahead.

Why caint they be like us? a ghostly man shouted, spilling his drink, which fell to the dusty floor. Cockroaches scuttled.

Randy couldn't breathe.

Gotta go, he said, and stumbled out of the bar. He had written that passage in his book. Those words had haunted many who had gone to live among the gringos.

Why caint they be like us? How does someone become someone else? And why should they? To get a job? To get ahead? To fit in? Out of fear?

Fear was the great assimilator.

And did the soul of the person change when the exterior changed? Wasn't the soul immutable?

Six

Randy meets Unica, who reminds him that only Jesus walked on water.

Randy made his way to the river and sat under a leafless cottonwood. Oso chased a chipmunk. The creature disappeared into a hole. Then he chased a big yellow butterfly, its butter-colored wings dripping with mystery.

Why had it not flown to Mexico with its kin? Would it die here? Was it following Darwin's law? Adapting. Or was the problem just a dumb protein gone haywire in its speck of a brain?

Not all individuals follow the laws of nature, Randy thought. They pay the price.

The cottonwood trees were the grandfathers of the river. The sacred trees of the region. Once they had provided shade for weary pilgrims in search of the fountain of youth, the hot springs. Now they provided homes for the great owls.

Randy chewed on a stem of dry grass and tried to remember the names of the three saints he was named after: Apolinario, Martín, Pantaleón . . . or was it Primitivo, Valentino, Fructuoso? No. Those had been the names of neighbors who visited his parents. Kind, hard-working farmers.

When? So long ago, it seemed.

He couldn't remember. He needed a *Book of Saints* to look up names. Maybe the priest could help. It didn't matter. Randy he had become and Randy he was.

Blue swallows darted along the surface of the water. Cutthroat trout swam languidly in the beaver pond. A few inches beneath the surface, a school of goldfish hung suspended, their feathered tails swishing ever so softly, lending consistency to the greater mystery of the universe.

Sunlight glistened on their golden backs. The finny-feathered friends became sunlight. Sun became fish. Photons. Light bending toward earth became fish. Without light there was no substance underneath. Or was there?

If light disappeared from the universe, would you bump into the table? Bump into God? That's funny, bumping into God in a universe void of light.

Black holes into which light disappeared.

If an atom be washed away into the dark sea of a black hole, it could not escape. Once past the event horizon, not even light could escape. But they said that not a speck of energy could be lost in the universe. All in perfect balance. Did the black hole create energy? Was God creating energy?

Randy had read that when a star collapses it creates a black hole. Agua Bendita was like a black hole in a far-away galaxy.

So it was with the fish. If they were not here at this exact moment, the universe would collapse. Every iota had to be at its exact place and velocity as the present time flowed into the far-flung future.

Así es, he whispered. That's the way it is.

The spell broke. A lovely green-and-blue dragonfly and its damsel alighted on a swaying reed. Piggy-back. The mating season had ended. They would soon be empty shells.

Was this the season of death?

The other side of the river looked peaceful. Skeletons of houses dotted the meadows at the foot of the mountain. Some-one lives there, Randy thought. Or spirits. His father had told him that long ago a native village had stood there. Adobe walls washed down by rainstorms dotted the area.

Sometimes in the evenings when the air was still, the spirit songs of the first natives could be heard. Deer browsing by the river paused to listen. Coyotes stopped yipping. The swallows flew epicycles to the beat of the drums. Bats darted in the dusk.

The nighthawk's flight announced the coming dusk.

At such times the place was magical. Pain and suffering were put on hold.

Smoke rose from chimneys. Maybe right now Sofia was out tending her lambs. Why couldn't he just walk across?

Only Jesucristo can walk on water, the old woman said. An old crone looking for roots and berries along the river had come up unexpectedly. Had she read his thoughts?

Buenos días le dé Dios, Randy greeted her.

Cada día es misterio del universo, she replied. O misterio de Dios. Es igual.

Did she mean God *is* the universe? The universe is God? Conscious? Alive? Aware?

You believe the universe is—

Stop right there, hijo, she cautioned. The universe *is*. That's all.

I thought only we humans were aware—

Bullshit! she replied, and sat next to Randy. Anda vamos a comer.

From her willow basket she took two baked sweet potatoes and watercress. She shared the food with Randy and they ate.

¿Cómo te llamas?

Randy.

Oh, a gringo name. Your granpo and gramma will not know you.

You knew them? Randy asked.

Pues, sí. I know everyone. I was here before the españoles.

Randy guessed she was from the pueblo. Legend had it that long ago during a battle with the españoles, some of the native women had jumped off the cliff. They sprouted wings like butterflies and landed safely. They still gathered nectar from the wildflowers in the meadows.

But now I don't care to remember, she said. On this earth I will never love again. They killed my parents, they killed my husband, and in the end they killed my children. May you never know such grief. No, on this earth I will never love again.

I'm sorry, was all Randy could say. He dared not ask details of the tragedy that had befallen her.

?Por qué? she said. Why? Memories bring back the pain, so I just invent the memories I want.

Randy wondered if he had known the old woman as a child. Had she visited his parents' home?

My father was Juan Diego Lopez, my mother Agapita.

Me llamo Unica. I am older than the angel who destroyed the bridge. His name was Espantoso. Muy cabrón. God sent him with an avenging sword, a sword of fire, y con un chingazo he destroyed the bridge. For crying out loud, for a moment we thought it was Jesus himself.

She made the sign of the cross. Now I cannot go visit my comadres on the other side.

In places the river is shallow. I could walk across—

!Zonzo! Didn't I just tell you? Only el Cristo walks on water!

Randy nodded.

She told the story of the river. Long ago this was el Río de las Golondrinas. The swallows sent water from the mountain. Up there was el Río de los Tecolotes. The owls stole corn from the Aztecs and brought us the seed. The bear, his name was Juan del Oso, dug a trench in the earth and created el Río del Oso. Swallows, owls, and bears were our vecinos. In those days the animals spoke to us. They brought water and corn. The americanos brought the potatoes. They were our vecinos.

Neighbors?

Sí, vecinos. Some were hard to get along with. But cranky neighbors don't belong only to the gringos, you know.

Randy knew. He had written that truth in his book.

Was there a cherry tree?

The old woman's eyes lit up. Yes! Because of the cherry tree Sofia can lose her virginity many times and still remain a virgin! We thought we lived in Eden.

But doesn't the Bible say it was an apple tree?

Bah! Those old prophets couldn't spell worth a damn! A woman with a cherry is much more beautiful than one with an apple. And more dangerous.

In his imagination Randy had to agree.

Sofia's father had a cherry tree, he said.

It's still there.

And Sofia?

Por supuesto.

And my father's house?

!Mira! She pointed. Everything as it used to be.

Randy peered into the mist and recognized his parents' home. A pomegranate tree grew in the yard. Papá y Mamá were sitting on the porch, shucking fresh ears of corn for supper. Talking softly about the day's work. *As it used to be.*

The image filled Randy with grief.

Why did you come?

To see them, to see everything . . . my childhood.

Did you look back? she asked.

No.

So you're *here*. The land of time-past is what you once knew. You only think you lived there. The present is an illusion that flows like water into the future. The future is all there is. And we don't know a damn thing about it. Así es. Present flowing into future and becoming *here*. She leaned close to Randy. *Here* is the land of Elsewhere. Clocks cannot measure our comings or our goings.

Elsewhere, Randy thought. Somewhere else. What did it mean?

But I feel time passing! Randy blurted. I saw a tarantula walk across the road, I fed my mare, the old man left to become bear scat, I ate a potato pancake—

You believe all that? Unica sighed. !Qué muchacho! Don't you know we make it up as we go along? You got to learn that.

Make it up as we go along. All of existence was like that. Why did he argue?

Unica looked into Randy's eyes.

I wish I could tell your fortune. What you do is what you become. I think you came for a purpose— The bridge! Yes! That's it! Didn't the book say a child shall lead them?

I'm not a child.

But you are inocente. An innocent soul. I will help you build your bridge! She stood.

How? Randy pleaded.

She pointed. Go to the forest and speak to the Singing Trees. Tell them you need their help.

Ask the trees for help? He felt puzzled.

Sí. The trees are dreaming they are a bridge. In that dream they transform themselves. That's all.

The image of trees becoming a bridge took shape.

I see, he muttered. !Gracias!

Hasta mañana, she said, and walked down the stream.

What are you looking for? Randy called.

Mandrake roots!

No one, not even the wisest curandera from the northern mountains, had ever found mandrake roots in New Mexico. The legend said that if a mandrake root was found in Agua Bendita a child would be born to Sofia of the Lambs. Was Randy the child waiting to be born? After all, the child is the father of the man. Unfortunately, no one in Agua Bendita understood what that meant.

The grief hounding Randy passed. Shivering, he lay against the trunk of a tree and thought about the bridge. Unica would help. Those he had encountered didn't remember him, but they would help. He wasn't alone in Elsewhere.

He smiled. Elsewhere. He liked that. At least he was here and not there.

The watercress made him burp.

He closed his eyes and fell into a deep sleep. Like Ali Baba. Or like Rip van Winkle.

In a dream, he crossed the river to Sofia's home. She gathered him in her arms and he fell asleep on her lap.

She sang a lullaby and stroked his curly hair.

> Duérmete niño lindo
> en los brazos de mi amor.
> Tú eres el sueño dulce
> de mi alegre corazón.

While resting on her lap, he dreamed he was out in the meadow helping her bring in the lambs.

In the dream he stumbled on the dry bones of an ancient creature, fell, and hit his head on a rock. He passed out and dreamed he had returned to his parents' home. They were overjoyed to see him. His mother called him by a name he didn't remember.

She fed him a big meal: calabacitas con maíz, beans, green chile, freshly baked tortillas, sweet arroz con leche. With lots of raisins, just like he liked it. After the meal she prepared his bed and he slept. He dreamed he was in his parents' home, sleeping and dreaming in the present tense.

Which dream would he awaken from?

Seven

Unica saves Randy from prior
dreams. He visits his godparents.
His padrino bemoans the loss
of the hispano land grants.

!Espera! Unica called.

He was about to open his eyes.

Quickly she deleted the prior dreams so that he would awaken under the cottonwood tree by the river in Agua Bendita.

?Qué pasa? ?Qué pasa? Randy cried, sitting up.

Unica explained, If you awaken from a dream within a dream, you will be in that place and not here. You should know that, tonto!

There's so much I don't know, he said, rubbing his eyes and looking around. He thought vaguely of the story of a Chinese man who dreamed he was a butterfly, and didn't know if he was a man or a butterfly when he awakened.

La vida es un sueño. También la muerte. Didn't you go to school? Didn't you read books?

Yes—

Bueno. Always delete the dream within the dream before you wake up.

Randy scratched his head. I don't know how to delete dreams.

You had a computer, didn't you?

Yes.

Hit the delete key. Delete what you don't need. Then log

off. Someday all our memories and dreams will be stored in a giant computer. All will be timeless again.

Pretty timeless here already, thought Randy.

Are there delete keys in dreams? he asked.

Of course, niño. Didn't your mother teach you?

They didn't have computers, he mumbled.

He had worked as a gardener for some ricos and saved enough money to buy a used laptop. He wrote *My Life Among the Gringos* on it. He and Oso were on their way to Santa Fe to show his book to a publisher when their express train hit a cow. The shock sent his laptop flying out the window. He remembered grabbing Oso.

Later, somewhat dazed, he had found himself on the road to Agua Bendita. He hadn't thought about the laptop till now.

Delete keys are okay if you control them. But sooner or later everyone gets deleted. La cabrona Muerte has the ultimate delete key. !Wáshale!

Unica laughed a throaty gurgle and went off grubbing for roots. Plenty of oshá, no mandrake, she whistled.

He felt in his pocket for his cell phone. It had also gone the way of the laptop.

Is there a telephone in town? he called.

?Pa' qué? No one to call, she answered and was gone. The mist that had suddenly swirled from the river had swallowed her up.

He could call someone. Who?

He had not married, had no children. Who would want to know where he was? He had moved from job to job, so there were no close friends. The thought was not pleasant.

Those few he had bumped into in time-past would go on with their lives. Memory was short-lived, and in the end his obituary would sound pretty dumb.

Here lies Randy Lopez. He took night classes. Claimed he wrote a book that was never found. Que descanse en paz.

Damn! Is that all?

His soul could not be described by those left behind. And that's all that was left after the fuse died and the flower wilted.

I'll show them. I'll write my own history.

That was some consolation. Take a little bit of memory from here, a little bit from there, and create who he was.

He wandered down the road. Oso followed. They arrived in front of a familiar house.

I know this house! Randy exclaimed. My padrinos live here. Come, Oso! Let's visit them. They'll remember me!

A garden of frost-eaten flowers filled the front yard of the small adobe home. The door and window frames were painted a lovely cerulean blue. Some said the tradition came from the Moors of Spain, others said that in heaven all doors are painted blue.

An old legend told how the Angel of Death could not pass through a door painted blue. The village pícaros laughed. Remember don Estevan? He painted his door blue, but he died anyway. Hung up his tennis shoes! Ya le tocaba.

They laughed. Cuando te toca, te toca.

Maybe La Muerte came in through the chimney, one of the pícaros suggested.

That's crazy! The neighbors laughed. La Muerte coming in through the chimney was just plain dumb! Only Santo Clos came down the chimney.

They went away laughing, but after a while a few blue chimneys begin to appear in Agua Bendita.

People begin to discuss a philosophy of blue. Just what was the right shade of blue to keep out La Muerte? People experimented. A man in Española made a fortune with his Blue

Dreams paint store. Even the lowriders begin to paint their car doors blue.

People went on dying.

¡Padrino! ¡Madrina! Randy called, and the old couple sitting on the porch looked up. They were wrinkled beyond belief, but Randy was sure he had found his godparents. They would know him.

Mateo! the old woman called. Mateo!

She hobbled to Randy, as did the old man. They hugged him and wet his shirt with tears so dry they evaporated before the sun hit them.

Mateo! they cried. ¡Hijo, qué gusto!

Randy appreciated the reception. They hustled him into the house, where his madrina offered him a slice of pastelito.

The old-fashioned homemade thick-crusted pies his mother used to bake had a prune or apple filling. With raisins. This was sweet potato pie.

When did you come?

Where were you?

Did you look back?

They cried again. Oh, Mateo!

Randy could keep silent no longer. I'm Randy, he said, looking into the rheumy, clouded eyes of the two.

Rando, the old man said. Randolfo?

No, Randy.

Ran-dee, they repeated, and looked at each other.

Is that a gringo name?

The two seemed displeased.

You baptized me! Randy protested. But you gave me the name of three saints no one can remember!

Válgame Dios, Madrina said. In those days we did not use the gringo names. I wanted to name you Melquiades.

I wanted to name him Zacarías like me, the old man said, clearly pissed off.

How did you become Randy?

The teacher . . . at school— Randy choked on the pie. It was stale, as if it had been on the table a hundred years.

You went to la escuela de los americanos. No wonder you changed. You don't belong anymore.

I do! Randy cried. I was born here! My father's house is here! It was heartbreaking to be met by his godparents and not be recognized.

So you lived with the gringos?

Yes.

What did you learn?

English—

So what? the old man sputtered. A bunch of monkeys with typewriters can type a Shakespeare play in a million years! You think I'm a fool? !Ten respeto!

Sí, padrino. I apologize.

So what did you learn? Padrino was clearly irritated.

Well . . . they're okay—

Bullshit! The americanos stole our land grants! You call that okay?

Yes, Padrino, but before that we took native land—

But we are natives! Indo-hispanos! I married Isadora from the pueblo! My father Cleofes married an indita from Santa Clara! She gave him a big family. Those were women! Us mestizos are all over the place!

Sí, Padrino. Randy knew. Maybe the time of the mestizo had arrived.

Some of the old people called themselves Indo-hispanos. Some said mexicano. When the americanos arrived, the kids in school were called Spanish Americans. Then Mexican

American, then Hispano, Chicano, Latino, on and on. Labels changing the exterior. The soul remained true to its history.

Destino. The concept was driven like a nail into the mestizo soul.

Yes! The time of the mestizo had arrived!

He took out his notebook. He had written about his life among the gringos. Had he been too soft on them? It was people like his godparents who first had to deal with the americanos when they had arrived in New Mexico. It had not been easy. Best not to hold back punches.

They prize aggression, Randy said lamely. But sometimes that's good, he added.

Bullshit! the old man thundered. We know prejudice when we see it! !Ay, Dios! he cried, and crumpled into a chair. Are we going to depend on the kids for the truth? God save us!

But things have changed, Randy said. There is more opportunity in the land of the gringos.

Try telling that to the poor mexicanos!

Some of my friends even married gringas.

Madrina made the sign of the cross. Ay, Dios.

Randy persisted. In the new global economy we will all be equal. No more prejudices—

Bullshit! Padrino retorted. If China goes, everybody goes! You better start learning Chinese!

We wish you well, Mateo, Madrina said. It was a struggle for us; it is a struggle for you. We know.

Randy knew it was time to go. But first he dared to ask his burning question: Do you remember me?

They looked closely at him. No, but we will bless you anyway.

He knelt, and they blessed him with fingers that crumbled into dust when they touched his forehead.

Eight

Randy meets the librarian and receives the book *How to Build a Bridge*.

Randy and Oso returned to the stable. In his heart Randy knew he was not going back, so he opened the gate and told the mare to go home. The mare nuzzled him affectionately, smelled Oso one last time, then went trotting down the road.

Tell Señor Todos Santos thank you! Randy called.

The mare whinnied and was gone.

There must be someone in Agua Bendita who remembers me, thought Randy.

Walking down the road, he met a woman pushing a cart full of books. Her stringy hair and the glasses sliding down her nose made her look like a librarian straight out of a Charles Dickens novel.

Excuse me, can I help?

The woman pushed the glasses up her perspiring nose and looked at Randy. This is my penance, she smiled, but I guess today I can share my labor.

A bag lady of books, thought Randy as he peered into her face. He recognized his old teacher Miss Libriana.

Miss Libriana!

Yes?

It's me, Randy!

Randy?

Yes!

Oh. One of the Garcia boys?

No.

You look like the Garcias.

Lopez. Randy Lopez. You named me!

Oh, I doubt that. I don't seem to remember.

Randy felt crestfallen. She didn't remember him. Perhaps it was the weight of gravity that addled her memory. Gravity seemed to be the only physical law still operating in Agua Bendita.

Randy remembered his teacher as a young woman— a breath of fresh air, shining hair, lively blue eyes, energetic, always smiling, and if she hugged you it was like heaven. Lilacs sprang beneath her feet and the aroma of the blossoms wafted around her. First grade had been heaven.

You taught me. I was in first grade. Remember?

I taught for many years, so many kids. When the Presbyterians came to the village they hired me to teach the Mexican children. The Presbyterians thought the kids should learn English and become Anglicized.

Anglicized. That meant to become like Anglos. White. But so many of the hispano kids were brown. How could they give up the color of their skins? Even in a democracy, color still mattered to some.

Of course culture was more than skin. It went deeper. It was a plethora of identity tags. Language. History. Legends. Music. The mythopoetic of a community. It meant pride in the ancestors and honoring their way of life.

Randy had explained Anglicized in his book. It was a euphemism for gringoized. But nobody liked the word gringoized. If you told a Chicano he was gringoized he would fight you. Even those who called themselves Latinos didn't like to be told they were gringoized.

Some who had become gringos and didn't know it just smiled.

More and more, Randy was beginning to believe that he should not use the word gringo. It was out of style. Why not use white? But *My Life Among the Whites* didn't make sense. White what? There were too many kinds of white, from progressive to reactionary. Besides. Hadn't Robinson Crusoe's accomplice written that book? Friday had lived among the whites.

There were white people who weren't white. Some of his own Chicano friends were fair-skinned, blue-eyed, and had blonde hair. What should they mark on the census forms? White. Not-so-white. Brown. Dark brown. What in the hell did Caucasian mean anyway? An empty concept.

He thought it was the French who had invented the word race. A bad move.

In Mexico a philosopher had named the offspring of Europeans and native people La Raza. The Europeans had conquered the natives, in the field and in bed. Genes mixed. La Raza was the progeny of that chingadera: the multicolored and multicultured Americas. A rainbow of colors. New World people. Nature's love of diversity. It was inclusive, like a fiesta. Anyone, but anyone, could show up.

It was difficult for Raza to be prejudiced against the next guy. He might be a primo.

Maybe the census should just ask: Poor, Not-So-Poor, Well-off. That might help spread the wealth a bit. Unfortunately, the Well-off would never agree.

Gringo is as good as any description, Randy resolved. Best keep it.

Randy's grandfather had told him that when the americanos arrived in New Mexico, the hispanos called them Griegos. Greeks. In other words, foreigners. Griegos became gringos. Ulysseus became Ulisis. Baklava became pan dulce.

So it went. Words changed pronunciation and thus meaning.

Now it was Spanglish. Chicanos mixed Spanish with English and communicated just fine. But Spaniards from Spain couldn't understand Spanglish. Ah well, most couldn't understand Basque, Catalán, Gallego. . . .

Let me help, Randy offered again. He took the handle of the cart and pushed. The books weighed more than the cross.

You do this every day? He puffed and dug his feet into the dry earth.

Yes. After the school closed, I turned it into a library. I had all the books in town. The classics. The whole world writ in books. Each day I roll the cart down the hill to the village plaza. I wait for folks to check out books.

Do they?

She laughed. No. Most of us are beyond reading. So I bring the cart back. I don't mind. It's all the love I have.

Randy remembered the path to the schoolhouse. When he glanced up, everything seemed in disrepair.

You should get help.

Oh, everyone's too busy looking after their own penance. Comes from the sins on each person's karmic wheel. She laughed again.

She hobbled along beside Randy. Lame from age and carting books up and down the hill.

Sins? Randy asked.

We all enjoyed them, she whispered. At one time or other.

Her breath came in gasps. Randy was afraid she would have a heart attack.

His own heart was pumping; his leg and arm muscles cried in pain. Each word weighed a ton, and there were millions of words in the books.

The classics are weighty, she said. Our legacy. Don't give up. Knowledge might save us in the long run.

He struggled with the books that no one read anymore. The knowledge of the world. The kids read very little anymore. Not even the new electronic books. The world of *time-past* had entered time-Elsewhere. Dumbed-down. Dictators would rule using the Internet.

Everybody was in Elsewhere, somewhere or other. For the moment Randy was glad he was here.

When he thought he could not take another step, they arrived. She opened the door and he pushed the cart into the dusty room.

I don't have time to clean, she apologized. But we do have time for tea. Then I have to start down again.

Randy fell exhausted into one of the desks. The very desk he had sat in long ago.

My desk! he exclaimed.

His initials were carved into the wood. Here is where he felt the first inkling of Sofia's love. She had been woven into the childhood stories he read, and he had fallen in love.

She was still here! In the books and in the musty air that held the dreams of children.

Sofia, he whispered, and reached out to touch her. The image evaporated.

Do you remember Sofia? he asked Miss Libriana.

Sofia of the Lambs? Not really. It seems I only remember what's in books. I guess you can call me a bookworm.

Long ago a carpenter had nailed crude shelves to the walls. They were bowed with the weight of many books. Yellowed pages from the old tomes fluttered to the floor. All was crumbling into dust.

I remember when the Presbyterians started this school.

Do you? What a sweet boy. What did you say your name—

Randy.

Lovely name. She served him a cup of tea and a stale potato cracker. She offered Oso a cracker but he refused it. He was getting tired of potato munchies.

I was baptized with the name of three saints, but you couldn't pronounce them. You called me Randy.

Forgive me, she said. Easier on the tongue than the Spanish names. The priest ran the old school. But all you learned was Spanish and catechism. Here you were given a name to fit the future.

Yes, Randy stammered, choking on the dry cracker. He thought of all the wonderful things he had done in the land of the gringos. He had learned a lot. But deep inside he felt a loss. What was it?

Are you well? she asked. He had grown pale.

Yes. Just thinking.

What are you going to do?

Build a bridge across the river.

What a wonderful idea! We haven't had a bridge since the church fathers blew it up. They said we should not know the other side. The world has continued divided. I think to be separated from each other is the greatest sin.

Yes, Randy agreed.

Maybe this will help. She dug in a pile of books and handed him one. *How to Build a Bridge.*

Randy took the thin, worn book. Thank you.

It's time for me to start back down. No rest for the wicked. Plus I get to enjoy the natural scenery as I go and come. It is beautiful here, don't you think? And so peaceful. The dead cannot be more grateful. As I push the cart, I have time to digest the thoughts in the books.

Can I help?

No, thank you. You have enough to do. Go build your bridge.

Exasperated, Randy grabbed her arm. It was you who named me! Don't you remember?

Her eyes grew sad. Time to confess. I knew the day would come, she whispered.

Why did you choose the name Randy?

I had a child, she said. His name was Randy. But I wasn't married, so the church fathers ostracized me. One day we were walking along the river. . . . She paused; tears wet her eyes. A sob escaped her lips— pale lips that had been shut from love for so long.

My son fell in. He drowned.

Oh, no, Randy groaned. He had heard the story of the drowned boy many times. The woman who cried for her child by the river's edge was La Llorona. The Crying Woman.

But hadn't La Llorona drowned her child intentionally?

Randy shivered. Had Miss Libriana become La Llorona? Was every woman a Llorona?

Once, on his way home late at night, he had heard La Llorona's chilling cry. Her ghostly figure appeared in the bushes. He ran home to his mother's arms.

I'll protect you, she had whispered. Be good. Obey your parents. Respect the old. She sang him the Songs of Virtues and he slept.

Later, he wondered if the Crying Woman's appearance had been a warning not to go live among the gringos.

What did you do? he asked with bated breath.

I said to myself, The next child who comes through the school door I shall name Randy. That must have been you.

Randy felt a heavy weight on his heart.

Time to go, she said, and stood to push the cart. Each day I do my penance. Don't we all?

Nine

Randy visits the post office, where four coyotes sit playing dominoes.

From where he stood, Randy could see Miss Libriana pushing the book cart down the hill. Going down was easier, but still a labor.

How many times a day did she come and go? All day? All night? There was a feeling of eternity mixed into the whole damn thing.

Was Agua Bendita the place described in the esoteric gospels? The outlawed gospel of John?

She had said she was doing penance. Why in the hell does anyone who is kind have to do penance?

He looked at the frosted river. It was running high. Cold-weather clouds hung over the mountain. Furious tumbling snowball clouds laden with ice.

A group of mexicano workers stopped at the river. The men carried bags of clothing and their tools. The women held babies on their hips. Older children clung to their skirts.

If they crossed they would continue north to el norte. The greater U.S.A., where there was work to be had. There was no work in Agua Bendita. There was no meat. Only potatoes, the food of the ancient Incas. The fruit that had punished the Irish and sent them across the sea. Some legal, some not.

The workers looked at the angry river and whispered, No se puede. They had crossed many rivers, and they judged this one treacherous. It ran furious and cold. They would not take chances with the women and children.

They turned away and went up the mountain into the trees. The children needed rest. They would eat cold potatoes. No campfires that might alert la migra.

On the other side of the river, Sofia wept silent tears.

Randy sighed.

The valley felt timeless in the bare sunlight. A scene from an ancient paradise. The old-timers used to say the river ran from Eden. Sacred water. Agua Bendita. Wasn't all water sacred? The stuff of life. Soon it would be more expensive than oil and horrific wars would be fought over it.

Maybe those wars had already begun, and that is why the earth was so dark and dusty. Nuclear arsenals exploding. Religion against religion. The Others blaming the Others.

Randy shivered.

Miss Libriana was out of view, but Randy was still thinking of her child. He had gotten his Anglo name from a drowned Randy. Well, he would carry it with pride. Did the name matter? After all, he had forgotten the names of the three saints.

It did matter! One would not call a rose by any other name. Call a rose a sunflower and it would protest. And vice-versa. Once the name was given, it became identity and pride. Naming was sacred. In the end, the name is inscribed on the tombstone.

How many souls had drowned in the sacred river? And was it safe to build a bridge? Had he bitten off more than he could chew? Was Sofia really the prize, or another illusion in his long life of illusions?

Randy whistled and Oso came running. The dachshund had been digging into prairie dog holes. Randy petted his dog. What a life.

He went down the road, and came to the village post office. The one-room building had been built by WPA workers.

Randy remembered his grandfather saying the WPA had saved the country. Poor people went to work. The president who initiated all those work projects was a saint to the country folks of Agua Bendita.

A couple of hispano families in the area had named their sons Roosevelt. Brown-skinned Roosevelts ran around the country. One became a teacher; the other wound up in prison.

So it goes.

Constructed from mountain granite, the post office sported a wood door carved by the famous woodcarver from Taos. The vigas that held the roof had been painted by men from the pueblo. Bright Zía suns, rain clouds, corn plants, a blue-and-green water snake encircling one of the timbers.

Randy remembered picking up the day's mail for his father. He loved the task, loved the rich aroma of the building, the importance of carrying home a letter or a Welfare check when there was no work.

A huge mulberry tree stood in front of the building. Under the dormant tree at an old card table sat four figures playing dominoes.

Randy rubbed his eyes. These were not men playing dominoes, but coyotes dressed as men. Their bushy tails swished back and forth under their chairs. They wore cowboy jeans, snakeskin boots, garish shirts and bright Pendleton jackets.

From time to time, one reached under the table for a jug of potato vodka, drank, and passed it around. Each smacked his lips after he drank, then the jug went back under the table and the game resumed.

The ranchers Randy had known as a boy had said the last wolves in the area had been killed in the 1920s. The last grizzly met the same fate. Those left fled north to Yellowstone. Only the coyotes remained. Shot at and poisoned, yet they survived.

Buenos días, Randy greeted the men. Coyotes. Oso made friends by sniffing around.

Hey, kid. New here?

What's your name?

Randy.

Randy dandy, said the first coyote.

Randy bandy, said the second.

Handy Randy, said the third.

Randy candy, said the fourth.

They laughed and chortled and gave each other high-fives.

Nice name, Randy. I once had a mule I called Randy.

They laughed again.

Another said, I caught a cabrón being randy with my wife, so I shot his ass.

Another burst of laughter, which would have continued had not the postmaster stepped out. A chunky man with thick arthritic hands. He had murdered plenty of letters and packages in his time.

Don mind them, he said. Things are slow. Damn e-mail ruined the PO. The Internet. All wireless—

Don't forget the delivery trucks! Cheaper than the PO. The coyotes laughed, pushed a few dominoes around, and passed the jug.

All day the dry berries of the tree rained down on the coyotes. They didn't seem to mind.

You new? the postmaster asked.

I was born here, Randy replied, wondering if this was the same man he had known as a child.

He looks like an Ortega, one of the coyotes offered.

No, a Sandoval.

Looks like a Moor to me.

You Catholic or Muslim?

My father was Juan Diego Lopez de la Cañada de Juan del Oso. Randy thought he had gotten his father's name correct. Had he? Or was he forgetting?

Oh, the postmaster nodded, rubbing his chin. They drowned when the angel destroyed the bridge . . .

Randy couldn't remember.

Pinche angel, a coyote murmured.

It wasn't an angel, his friend argued. It was the reactionary government secret forces. They don want us knowing what's on the other side.

It was bombed during La Guerra de Pan Duro, another said.

The War of Hard Bread. I forgot what bread tastes like.

Remember hard tortillas?

Oh, yeah. Us coyotes know hard times.

Do you remember me? Randy asked.

No. But you look like a Márquez. They was gamblers. They loved horse races. Lost everything they owned at the casino.

He don smell like them, one said.

How do you know what they smell like? his partner asked.

Slept with his wife!

That set off a boisterous round of laughter that spilled the dominoes on the ground.

Me pescaron en la mora, one said. They caught me picking mulberries. Got home with stained hands. He brushed the wrinkled mulberries off his jacket. My wife will know where I've been.

Those stains last forever, his friend said. Like original sin. Or pomegranate juice. He winked at Randy.

Maybe your old lady's gonna be at the casino when you get home.

Caint! I hid her credit card!

They laughed anew.

Wait a minute, the postmaster interrupted. Did you say Lopez?

Yes.

Had a pomegranate tree?

Yes! Randy exclaimed.

Come inside. I got a stack of letters . . .

Randy followed him into the musty building. Cobwebs hung from the ceiling. Mice scattered when Oso entered.

Dust-covered packages were stacked to the ceiling. Letters bulged from crammed niches. All sorts of tattered boxes covered the once-brilliant Saltillo tile floor.

The postmaster reached into a dark corner and retrieved a small, dusty bundle. Aquí está.

He handed the bundle to Randy. Yours, aint they?

Randy looked at the faded letters. Yes. His return address. He had written to his parents— and love letters to Sofia!

They had not been delivered. Disappointment filled Randy's heart.

Gracias, he said, holding the tattered letters to his heart. His parents and his Beloved hadn't received his messages.

Don take it so hard, kid, the postmaster said. Most of us here caint read. Maybe used to.

Todo se acaba, one of the coyotes yawned outside.

On this earth nothing lasts, everything ends. It was a common refrain the old nuevo mexicanos used. Years of hard work weighed heavy on the shoulders and the heart. The body grew tired, diseases gnawed at the flesh, depression destroyed the soul.

Todo se acaba. Everything ends, the old people whispered. This truth kept them close to God.

Randy thanked the postmaster and said goodbye to the coyotes. They paid no attention. The potato vodka had put them into a deep, snoring sleep.

He went to the river and opened the envelopes. The ink was faded; his words of love had disappeared. Nothing lasts. One by one he slipped the letters into the rushing water.

Was the past dead? Was there nothing to hold on to?

Ten

—

Randy meets Angelica, who keeps the tortured children of the world.

Randy followed the road to the playground. He and his childhood friends had spent many an afternoon here. During summer after baseball, swimming, or fishing, they hung out at the swings. It was a place to meet the village girls.

Now the see-saw and the swings were rusted. Weeds covered the grounds.

A woman with red-stained lips and hair the color of gold sat in a swing. Her many children played in the nettle-infested field.

How strange, thought Randy. The children are multicolored: red, white, cinnamon, black, blue, yellow, and some bruised like apples after a hail storm. Those badly crippled sat forlorn, neither moving nor talking.

The woman must be a siren, the kind that bewitched Ulysseus on his way home to Ithaca. See how she stares at the river as though it were the wide Sargasso Sea.

Best move on, thought Randy. He started, but she called good morning in a voice so sweet it was answered by a warbling melody from the mockingbirds.

Not a siren, but an angel whose hair fell to her mud-stained feet. The children looked up.

Good morning, Randy replied.

Someone had put the thought in his mind that he had not really come to Agua Bendita, but to limbo. So that's what he thought now. These are the babes of limbo playing in the brambles until the doors of heaven open to receive them.

I'm Angelica, the woman said. It was freezing in the night but it's getting warm. Thank God for the sun. Mankind's greatest fear is for eternal darkness to come over the earth. Imagine the sun going dark. Complete panic. No sun the second day, and the world falls apart. People die of fear. Then imagine forty days and forty nights of darkness. Everything disappears.

You might bump into God in the dark, Randy said. So he believed.

God is Light. Even She would disappear.

Damn, thought Randy. That's depressing. I don't want to think about it.

He sat under the lone juniper tree. Oso ran to play with the children.

My dog playing with angels. What next?

I'm Randy.

Glad to meet you, Randy. I'm Angelica. On your way to the fiesta?

Yes, Randy lied. He had heard the music from the fiesta and would go there. But first he wanted to find someone who remembered him.

You from around here?

I used to live here.

Really? I thought you might be a magician. Todospedo the mayor invited magicians. They're gypsies from Spain. The duendes dance and juggle balls and make things disappear and appear again. Can you do that?

Randy smiled. No, I'm no magician.

Are you a dancer?

No, I don't dance.

Do magic tricks with cards?

No.

What *do* you do?

I'm looking for someone who remembers me.

Estás loco, she said, but with a smile so sweet that he took no offense. Come on, what do you do?

I wrote a book, he replied.

Ay, muchacho, there's no sense in writing books. People don't read anymore.

I know, Randy said.

He had taken night classes to learn to write, and that's all the teacher had talked about: the death of the book. By this she meant all books yet to be written. Old books would remain in libraries where only crusty old scholars would read them. New books would be electronic impulses.

I used to read, she said, and wiggled her mud-stained toes to get his attention. Her thin skirt slipped up to her knees.

What beautiful knees, thought Randy, and looked away. She was lovely, her smile beckoning, her eyes lively as sparklers on the Fourth of July.

What's your book about?

My life among the gringos—

You mean Anglos, she corrected him. It's nicer.

Yes, Randy agreed. My ancestors called the Anglos who came to Agua Bendita los americanos. But they weren't all Anglos. Some were Presbyterians.

She laughed. Oh, God, there were more than Presbyterians. There were all kinds. Methodists, Baptists, Jewish merchants, hippies. And the Texans! You want a dynamite story, you try pinning them down.

You're right, Randy said. He had forgotten about the Texans. Maybe they were the original gringos.

Angelica told the history: The old nuevo mexicanos welcomed the early fur trappers, who sold them rifles. Later the Jewish merchants arrived and sold them cast iron pots and calico dresses. They set up stores where the women could buy sugar, lard, flour, and rolls of cloth. St. Louis merchandise arrived in Agua Bendita and the people bought.

But the Texans! she exclaimed. Nobody loved the Texans. They brought grief. They fenced the land with barbed wire. They didn't like Mexicans. It took centuries to get over those prejudices, and some aren't done yet.

Randy nodded. He knew the history.

It's the children who suffer, she said sadly.

He looked at the children playing tag with Oso. Yes, it was the children who suffered the past injustices. And the present.

Randy cleared his throat and told the version he had heard: During the war with Mexico, the American soldiers who invaded Mexico sang a tune: Green Grow the Lilacs. The mexicanos said, Here come the green grows. Thereafter, the americanos were called gringos. Later other labels appeared: Bolillos. Gueros. Gringos salados. Gabachos.

And the gringos had labels for the mexicanos: Greaser. Beaner. Wetback. Pancho. All words have a history. Every group has a name for the other group.

But the word gringo is really innocuous, Randy said. It originally meant the americanos. They spoke a language the mexicanos couldn't understand.

That was long ago, Angelica said. Now everybody's the same, except those who aren't.

That's why I thought if I wrote about my life among the— excuse me, the Anglos, it might make a good book.

Where did you learn to write?

I took night classes. I bought a used laptop and wrote a novel. My instructor said I was pretty good, so I kept writing.

Pretty good doesn't cut the mustard anymore, she said.

Randy blushed. It was true. Who would read his story? Maybe the time of the gringo was over. Maybe the world was beginning to accept its multicultural nature.

Angelica . . . do I know you?

Maybe. I been here ever since—

When?

She looked puzzled. The children. Someone has to take care of them.

They're yours?

Mother nature's gift. The village boys used to come here in the evenings. They would sweet-talk the girls.

Something in Randy's heart went thump. He felt a rush. This was the Angelica he had known. He remembered the cool summer evenings when the village boys met the girls at the playground. A lot of small talk and giggling.

The older boys took girls walking along the river. They sat on the sweetgrass by the river's edge. Later some had to get married. Or the boy ran off and joined the army.

He had taken Angelica for a walk. She was his first love! But it wasn't love. It was just the way their bodies had felt. The Devil makes the flesh get hot, the priest had said. Jump in the cold river and drown the Tempter.

Temptation. The world was full of temptations. A high percentage of people loved it that way.

Are you real? Randy asked. It was the question he had been dying to ask.

She laughed. What do you think?

And the children?

My spiritual children. They're children of the river. Girls couldn't go home pregnant.

Randy looked toward the cold gray river.

They're all colors, he said.

Colorful, she smiled. Just like humanity.

The bruised ones?

Abuse, wars, genocide, abortions, diseases, hunger . . . their spirits reflect their suffering.

They look cold. They need jackets.

Angelica sighed. The world didn't provide.

She was their guardian. Here at last they knew some kindness.

Randy sat in silence, listening to the children play. They chased Oso, laughing joyfully.

They love your doggie, she said.

I'm Randy Lopez. I sat three desks behind you in art class. You were always drawing children. You won a prize at the state fair.

Yes, she smiled. My family was so excited we went to town. We drove back singing old songs like Billy Boy and Cielito Lindo. But freak accidents happen. There was a drunk driver on the road . . .

Randy nodded. I remember, or he thought he remembered. He was beginning to make up memories to fit the situation. Just like Unica said. He had thought only old people made up memories. No, it was a human condition.

Do you remember me? We lived down by the river. My father had a pomegranate tree in the front yard. The kids stole the fruit when it was ripe.

Too bad, she said. They paid for that. We thought your father was a brujo. He let us steal the forbidden fruit.

No, Randy protested. You're thinking of the apple in the garden. Adam and Eve.

No. Not the apple. It was pomegranates. I remember the tart

red juice. We spit out the seeds. It stained like blood. Like mulberries when they're ripe. We were marked for sure.

So you do remember!

Yes.

And you remember me?

Who?

Randy! Randy Lopez!

She looked at him with sadness in her heart and shook her head. No, I'm truly sorry, but I don't.

Randy studied her closely. Her red lips . . . she had eaten the fruit. And the stains on her feet were not from mud, but from the juice of the pomegranates!

Eleven

Randy visits the cemetery and meets the Devil.

The Catholic camposanto is on the hill by the church, she said. The conversos are also buried there. I guess even in death they're still trying to prove to their neighbors that they are muy católicos. Presbyterians have their own cemetery. Baptists I guess are raptured straight to heaven, at least those saved. I don't know about the Jewish ossuaries.

She paused, then continued.

Hindus and Muslims never arrived in Agua Bendita. Maybe the name discouraged them. We tried to be ecumenical by changing the name to Hot Springs. After that a few Methodists arrived. And a few free-wheeling Unitarians. All are welcome.

Oh, a Zen master came. He sits by the hot spring and contemplates his navel. He bathes often. His mother must be very proud of him.

Different cemeteries, Randy pondered. Even in death we are separated.

Yes. In Texas a while back they refused to bury a Mexican American veteran in a white cemetery. He died for the country but he couldn't lie by them in death.

I remember, Randy said. Those things happen.

Those things happened to my children. They bear the scars. Some are so traumatized they can't move. Mira. She pointed at the children with withered, frozen limbs.

Terrible, Randy said. Can I help?

Too late, she whispered. The world didn't take care of its children.

Randy felt chilled. I gotta go, was all he could say. Thank you.

De nada. See you at the fiesta. I'm taking the kids to ride the merry-go-round.

Randy started up the hill to the cemetery, where he thought he might find his parents' tombstones. Oso chased a roadrunner that looked like it had sprung out of a book.

Beep beep. Randy smiled. He knew Oso would not hurt the dancing roadrunner.

The dull sun was warming a little. It glistened on the flint and volcanic rocks of the hill. The dark flint was sharp and dangerous for Oso's sensitive paws. Randy picked him up.

Grrra-sas, Oso purred.

Long ago the natives had used flint to make knives. Piedra lumbre. A rock that made fire. The earth was made from fire. Lucky for evolution there was also water. The first cells fermenting in dark ponds. Then desire. Without desire there was nothing.

The four elements of antiquity made the man. That and a smattering of minerals and electricity. But you had to add desire to the melting pot.

And soul. What of the soul? Whence? God-sent? That's what he had been taught. Now he wondered. Was the soul desire? The Breath of Life given by God and taken by God? Was that all? Did desire die?

The place felt forlorn. Malpaís. Bad ground. Randy swore that if he stayed long enough he would remove all the rocks and plant grass. A cemetery should have grass and trees. Shade for the spirits.

Might that become his penance? he wondered. Best let the

priest take care of the camposanto. And the cross.

He arrived at the first row of tombstones. Simple white-washed crosses that shone in the sun. Headstones made from cement were all the villagers could afford. They poured the wet concrete in a simple form and scratched in the name of the departed.

No marble. There were no ricos in Agua Bendita.

He read the names of the most-recent dead.

Ortiz, Sandoval, Pino, Saavedra, Gómez.

The church bell rang. Una mujer con un diente, llama toda la gente. A woman with one tooth calls all the people.

A row of old women dressed in black wound up the hill to the church. Like crows. Or spirits seeking redemption.

He paused. The names and dates were faded, erased by wind, rain, and sun. Where did his parents rest?

What was he looking for anyway? Some assurance that he had indeed been born in Agua Bendita? If he couldn't find his parents' names on the crumbling tombstones, could he be sure?

Why did I come home? Why?

The question scraped his heart. Muscles twitched.

He moved on to the second row, crosses made from wood, worm-eaten and gray. Rotten at the core. If he touched them they crumbled. The names of the deceased had been burned into the wood with a hot blacksmith's iron. Black ash. Like the bodies buried beneath.

He read the names: Luna, Gutiérrez, Chávez, Montoya, Márquez. On and on. A couple of Anglo names scattered about. One Irish. McIntosh. One of the few Catholic gringos who had come to live with the hispanos of Agua Bendita. Where was this man's progeny? Had he written a memoir about his life among the nuevo mexicanos?

Did he learn to eat beans and chile? Tortillas? Menudo?

I'll check the Internet when I get back, Randy thought. Back where? Maybe there was no turning back. That's why those he met kept asking did you look back.

The rows of crosses went up the hill. Here was written the history of the village. The wood crosses of the first settlers were dust now. Up on the mesa the bones of the original natives blew in the wind. Dinosaur bones lay buried beneath, the denizens of earlier epochs. The earth abides.

He picked up a wood cross. Levi Rael. He turned it over. Burnt into the back was the Star of David. So Father Polonio was right about old Levi. Converso.

Levi could have written a book: *My Secret Life Among the Catholics.* Sooner or later everyone could write about his or her life among the Others. Always the Others. Why?

A man coughed. Randy turned. A thin, bent old man stood staring at him. The oldest man Randy had ever seen. Older than fire. Wizened eyes. Fiery eyes, clotted with gray matter. A cough rattled in his throat when he spoke.

?Quién es? Randy asked.

Soy El Demonio, the man replied.

Randy trembled. !El Demonio! The Devil! !Chingao! What did I do wrong?

Randy figured the Devil spoke French, so he said, Bon jour.

I speak all languages, the Devil smiled.

Oso whimpered. He would not sniff the sulfurous stranger.

I'm Randy. He shook the old man's hot hand.

I know, the Devil replied. I know all names. Past, present, and Elsewhere.

Oso growled a warning. Be careful, master.

What do you— why are you here?

Here? the Devil replied. I'm everywhere. The world is my

domain, as I told your Jesucristo. Tibo dabi— I offered him the world. He wouldn't take it. Talked about saving mankind and all that malarky. All those old prophets get like that sooner or later. Rant and rave about saving the worms. Desert sun burns their brains, I guess.

Randy gulped. They say, el diablo sabe—

Sabe todo por ser viejo, no por ser diablo. I know, I know, spare me the folk wisdom. I am old. I preceded God. He was the Word, the Logos, but I was the narcissistic Thought in his brain. A priori.

You preceded—

In the beginning was the Thought. Presuming the Thought preceded the big bang. Actually it makes no difference to me. I've always been around. But I didn't come to talk philosophy. The world is full of such mumbo-jumbo. And they make me out to be evil. Ridiculous! How can I be evil if I live in the soul of every man?

I don't understand.

Let me put it this way. I am the constant guest. I am in you. You're not evil, are you?

No, Randy gulped. He could smell the sulfur, see the flint rocks melting at the Devil's cloven feet.

I was on my way to the fiesta, the Devil said. It's Día de los Muertos. My favorite holiday. He laughed and spit hot phlegm.

Randy didn't appreciate his humor. Could he trust the Deceiver? His parents had warned him the Devil tells many lies.

Come on. Don't be so serious. Let's party.

Randy breathed a sigh of relief. The fiesta *was* a party! The man was wearing the mask of the Devil. He wore a costume for the fiesta. That's it! A costume!

Let's walk together. The Devil slipped his arm under Randy's. I'll keep you warm.

What choice did Randy have? What choice does anyone have? Sooner or later a person has to choose: Walk with the constant guest or not.

You say you abide in the soul, Randy muttered. I find that hard to swallow. Not all of us are devilish.

Good and evil abide in everyone. If God is in you, so am I. One cannot escape the paradox. And if I was the Thought before the Logos, well then, doesn't that make me first in place? The Prime Mover and all that.

I thought you were just a phantom our parents used to frighten us. Like El Coco or La Llorona. Behave, have good manners, don't stay out late, or El Demonio will get you.

The Devil laughed. Parents are funny. Sometimes ridiculous. I am that dark presence in your soul. It's that simple. Anda, vamos. I hear they're serving potato beer at la fiesta.

They walked down to the river arm in arm, like old friends, conversing as they went.

Randy carried Oso. The small dog had no concept of God or the Devil. Good and evil didn't exist in his dog brain. His true nature was to love and protect his master.

Still, he could smell the sulfur. And it doesn't come from a lit match, Oso thought. Like when you use the toilet then light a match. Best keep my distance.

Twelve

The Devil introduces Randy to La Muerte. The old bitch explains the Roots of Life.

They went down the hill to the fiesta. Dust rose from the dancing, shrouding a stand of ancient, skeletal mulberry trees.

The babes of limbo, angelic heads with wings, buzzed around the trees, eating the dark, dried berries. They made a humming sound, like swarming honeybees.

Randy stopped. Do you see what I see?

I know, I know, the Devil replied. They don't belong to me. They'll get their just reward by and by. If you believe that malarky.

Malarky seemed to be his favorite put-down.

The festivities had reached a feverish pitch. The earlier sacred music of the Matachines had been replaced by carnival music. A small Ferris wheel and merry-go-round cranked away. Angelica's children rode endless rides.

Just like the católicos, the Devil said. Any excuse for a party. They have a saint's day for every day on the calendar. Why? So they can party. Even the priest is here. The pícaros call him El Jefe. Jefe de muchos, if you ask me. When he's not hearing confessions, he's partying.

Randy looked. There was crippled Father Polonio dancing a vigorous polka with a top-heavy woman. Her mascara and eyeliner had run down over her heavily rouged cheeks.

What a clown!

Did he mean the priest or the woman?

Maybe he came to bless the fiesta, Randy said lamely. His parents had taught him to respect priests.

Yeah, right! the Devil scoffed. Blessing the fiesta! Duck feathers!

Duck feathers! he repeated, and a fit of laughter bent his thin frame. He coughed and spat. The stuff burned the grass at his feet. It was obvious he had been drinking.

Santo Niño, he sputtered.

Randy looked surprised. You can say the holy names?

I can say any name! Who do you think I am?

El Demonio, Randy answered, stepping back.

!Sí! !Cuídate! !Ten respeto! He exhaled sparks and smoke. I can say any name in the holy book, from A to Z!

The Bible? Randy asked.

No! The Book of Life. You are slow, muchacho. Lots to learn. He pointed. Here comes my comadre, La Muerte. The old bitch in drag. I'll introduce you. She can teach you a thing or two about life. Muy cabrona.

They wandered into the thick of things. Natives selling clay pots and silver necklaces. Turquoise bolo ties. Potato tamales and potato chips. Fermented potato beer that gave off a stench.

Randy remembered. I used to go to fiestas with my parents. My father knew many of the natives. They were our vecinos. He traded apples for corn. In spring they cleaned the acequia together. How I wish I could be there again.

Forget there, the Devil said. No one has ever gone from here back to there. Look. Even the Presbyterians showed up. He pointed at a group dancing and drinking potato vodka. And the Baptists selling Gideon Bibles. Raising funds to send their kids to camp. All's fair in love and war. I see the Methodists have stayed away.

The Zen master was also enjoying himself. The thin brown man was dancing with Kali, smiling widely, dragging his saffron robe in the mud. The people clapped to the tambourine rhythm and egged him on.

Randy couldn't believe his eyes. A few colorful streamers hung in the trees and over the booths. A band played. Mariachis had been hired. Couples spontaneously jumped up and danced. The old, the infirm— and even those who looked like Posada's cartoon death-figures jiggled their hips.

El Baile de los Viejitos, the Devil said. He laughed.

Randy smiled.

Was this a day of respite in Agua Bendita, or was every day a fiesta? A never-ending fiesta. Was there more to come?

Just about everyone is here! Randy exclaimed.

The whole world is represented, said the Devil. We are democratic like that.

It was true. Randy spotted the seven vices. And the four horsemen of the apocalypse. La Llorona. Grendel. Tiresias the soothsayer. Greek heroes. Quixote and Sancho. Lady Godiva on her white horse. Hordes of the unfaithful dragging the trappings of their sins behind them. Generals and madmen who made war, all crippled by their own insanity. Scholars and fools. Some scholars making fools of themselves. Several frail figures with bleeding stigmata. None with five.

Imposters, said the Devil.

La Muerte approached. !Querida! the Devil called. !Oye, vieja! Honey! Aquí estámos. !Ven acá!

Randy studied the strange figure that approached. She was dressed in a bright purple gown that trailed in the dust and a hot pink feathery scarf that also dragged. High heels obviously from a charity store, one heel broken so it made her limp. Eyeliner so thick she looked ghoulish. Her hair teased up like the old pachucas of the 1940s. She held a pair of rusted scissors in one hand and waved with the other.

¡Viejo! ¡Amor mío! ¡Guapo! ¡Ahí voy!

The goth kids would love her outfit, thought Randy.

Flaming orange lipstick, loads of dangling earrings, and nose rings and tongue studs that made her lisp. Every finger loaded with rings. All cheap jewelry.

She wears a ring on every toe, the Devil whispered. And on all her nipples.

All? You mean—

Many, the Devil answered. The young love her milk. Also those who make war. Kids racing their cars adore her. Not the old. For them her milk is sour.

Randy chuckled. That's not La Muerte.

Shhh! the Devil warned. She's sensitive.

Death approached and embraced the Devil. ¡Diablo! ¡Guapo! ¡Qué gusto me da!

You're looking good, vieja.

Y tú, viejo. There's a sparkle in your eyes.

Seeing an old flame like you makes me sparkle. He took her hand and gallantly kissed it.

¡Ay, carajo! You make me feel so good!

You're the best, you vamp! You look like a million.

Years old! Death laughed. How do you like my outfit?

A.T.M., the Devil winked— ¡A toda maquina!

They kissed in the French style, one then two loud smacks on each cheek.

Where do you keep yourself? the Devil asked.

The wars keep me busy. Darfur, Iraq, Afghan, Palestine. Muy ocupada. My scissors have worn dull. I need a helper. Maybe La Santa Muerte will show up. Do you know some of la gente treat her like a saint? ¡Están locos!

Randy knew La Santa Muerte was not really a saint. Some mexicanos had begun calling her a saint and dressing her in the traditional robes of La Virgen de Guadalupe. The poor prayed to her, hoping she would help their sons escape the wrath of the drug cartels. Sons who died daily in the insidious drug trade.

I'm here to party! La Muerte cried. Let's dance!

In a while. Mira. I want you to meet my friend Randy. Looking for a purpose in life.

Better late than never, Death said and smiled, revealing a pair of choppers that would make any bad boy pee his pants.

What a handsome young man! She shook Randy's hand. Her bones felt cold. Welcome to la fiesta! Wanna dance?

No, Randy stuttered.

Are you afraid?

Randy nodded.

You have nothing to fear, hijito, Death assured him. Ya lo que pasó, pasó. But I am at your service.

The comment set the Devil and La Muerte to laughing uproariously. At your service, they kept repeating.

Their easy way and laughter made Randy relax. The gaiety of the fiesta lightened his mood. He had felt spells of dread since he entered the village. But now the music and the dancing lifted his spirits.

And the Devil and Death were friendly. Actually funny.

You look puzzled, La Muerte said.

I . . . I thought you were fatter—

Fat! Death exclaimed. Don't insult me! Thin is in! The government wants to get rid of obesity. Fewer calories! Less diabetes. !Entre más flaca más dulce el hueso!

At this both the Devil and Death fell into another laughing

fit, slapping their knees and drawing the attention of those nearby.

Randy protested. But my grandfather said you eat people. So you should be fat!

Ay, hijito, your abuelo had it all wrong. Sit here and I'll explain. They sat on crates of rotting potatoes.

Let's see how I can explain my job. It's this way. Picture a beautiful sunflower. If worms eat the roots, the sunflower falls to the ground. The stalk, leaves, and flowers eventually rot and become compost. But while it bloomed the sunflower created beauty. That beauty cannot die. It joins the greater beauty in the universe and goes on spinning.

I see, Randy nodded, not quite sure where this was going. So you're like the worm?

Exactly. With these scissors I cut the Roots of Life.

The Roots of Life? I don't understand.

It's like this. Every person since birth is rooted to the earth. The earth is life. When I cut the roots the person dies. The Breath of Life leaves the body. The body returns to earth, buried or cremated. The soul goes on spinning into the greater consciousness. Neither the flesh nor the soul can be destroyed. Flesh becomes earth-dust, soul joins the Universal Soul.

It's a never-ending process, the Devil added.

She hugged the Devil. Gracias, amor. Tú sabes todo.

Por ser viejo, he smiled.

Transformation, Randy mumbled.

Yes! *Here.* A place you once knew and loved, La Muerte said. It's like this, Randy. The flower that grew in earth is part of the planet earth. Everything is born of earth, water, and a few minerals. The flower creates beauty that becomes part of beauty in the universe. Same with people.

Randy pondered the meaning. So my roots connected me to life?

Yes. Connected you to earth. You are an earth creature. You have a little bigger brain than other creatures, that's all.

I see, Randy whispered.

Good! Death exclaimed, and gave him a high-five. All I do is cut the roots, but I certainly don't eat the flesh. And I never said I take the soul. I'm just a servant in the mystery of life.

Not even I can take the soul, the Devil said.

What? Randy exclaimed. But I thought you took people to—

Hell? Oh, no. Those are stories people tell about me. Se lo llevó el diablo. The Devil took him. Nonsense! I scare kids, but I can't take anyone. I have no home. I wander the earth. I see everything that happens, but I don't create the evil in the world. Mankind does a pretty good job of that.

We get bad press, La Muerte said.

Yes, the Devil agreed. The more a man sins against his fellow men, the more he blames me. Depressing. I feel like a drink. Anda, comadre. Let's have a glass of beer. Lift our spirits. Join us, Randy?

No, thank you. I have a lot to think about.

Don't think too hard, Death said. Here comes a pretty girl. Got any money? Pretty girls will spend your cash!

!Algo es algo, dijo El Diablo! She looks muy liberated. And where there is sexual liberation, democracy will follow.

Yup. You don't need laws. Sex is its own constitution.

They laughed and arm in arm went off to the beer booth, dissolving into the cloud of dust the partygoers raised with their dancing.

Thirteen

Randy meets Mabelline, who fancies herself the Cleopatra of Agua Bendita.

The young woman who approached was dolled up in an Egyptian outfit. Like the one Liz Taylor wore in the movie. Exposing fine attributes. On her head the asp crown.

Randy thought she must be a prostitute. Flashy and trashy, but she did exude an aura of beauty. He had read the myth of Isis. She had fished her brother's body parts out of the Nile. The River of Life for the ancient Egyptians.

Isis sewed Osiris's body parts together. A myth far older than the Frankenstein story.

In the movie Liz Taylor rode a fabulous barge down the river. The Egyptian myths told of a barge for the dead. There was no bridge across the Nile.

What did the Devil say? the woman asked Randy.

He said there's already a bridge across the river.

And?

I looked and sure enough, there was a shining bridge of gold and precious stones. Diamonds, pearls, opals, and Chinese jade.

You can't believe the Devil.

I know, Randy agreed. My parents taught me to stay away from him. Go to church. Say your prayers. Respect your elders and help the poor. No andes con mala compañía. Keep away from bad people.

Dime con quién andas y te digo quién eres, she said. You are known by the company you keep. And there you were, hanging out with the Devil and La Muerte.

Randy blushed. How true. You are known by the company you keep. He had lived in the land of the gringos, ergo— had he become one?

The Devil lies, the woman said.

Yes. When I looked again the bridge had disappeared. An illusion. La Muerte told the Devil to quit pulling my leg. They were joking.

Poor kid. She touched his cheek. As sweet a jolt of electricity as he had ever felt. It made him yearn for more.

You know when you meet the Devil you're supposed to make the sign of the cross. Place your thumb over your forefinger and say, Póngote la Cruz!

I did, Randy replied. But I couldn't do it to his face. He seemed so friendly. I kept my hand in my pocket.

That's why it didn't work. And La Muerte. What did the old bitch say?

Some philosophy about the Roots of Life I didn't understand. By the way, I'm Randy. He took her hand and an aroma of lust and apricot blossoms filled the air.

I'm Mabelline.

Mabelline! He had gone to school with Mabelline. Scruffy knees, bucktoothed, nose always running, shoes full of holes.

I remember you! Randy gushed.

A lot of guys do. She smiled.

Your dad had milk cows. He sold milk and cheese.

And I delivered, Mabelline said. God those were hard times. Freezing in winter and melting in summer.

Randy couldn't believe his eyes. But you changed, he sputtered.

Who hasn't?

How did you—

Get from there to here? Maybe drinking all that organic

milk. She laughed and glistening pearls rolled from her lips. No, really, it's a matter of transformation.

I don't get it, Randy said.

All of life is becoming something else. Nothing is standing still. What you see now changes a second later. Like stepping into the river— same river but take the next step and it's not the same river. Get it?

Yes. Randy had heard that story. But what did it really mean?

We are always becoming. Especially here. That's the secret of life. Or of death, as La Muerte would say. You can't have one without the other.

Randy thought of the old man riding up the mountain on the Appaloosa. To become bear scat.

So that's what happens here, Randy said.

It happens all over, Mabelline replied. It's a law of the universe. Don't you remember science class?

Yes, Mr. Montoya . . . the science teacher! It's all coming back! Energy can't be created or destroyed. Something like what La Muerte said. An invisible root is cut, the body returns to the earth— bear scat!

Bear scat? Mabelline looked puzzled.

And the soul just goes on spinning! Becoming something new!

Mabelline shrugged. You want to party or not?

Yes, science class! Randy cried, throwing his arms around her knees, knees so well-shaped and lovely that many a man had met his downfall just by looking at them. To dream of such knees was to court orgiastic pleasures unknown even in the land of the Cama Sultry.

Don't you remember me from science class?

What did you say your name was? she asked, feeling a bit violated by the way he held her.

Randy! Randy Lopez! I used to live three houses from your dad's dairy! I saw you pass every day on the way to school! I didn't know you would become a goddess of love! he finished on the verge of tears.

Poor child. I just don't remember you. Sit here.

They sat on a box of rotting potatoes and she stroked his curly hair. Poor child, she repeated, holding him against her luxurious bosom.

He felt sorrow. For a moment he thought he had finally met someone who remembered him.

Ay, niño. Maybe I do remember you. We used to go on science trips to the river. We caught salamanders and cut off their tails. They grew back. You took me under the mulberry tree. It was you, wasn't it?

Randy cried, No, no, no! She had been a scrawny milkmaid. He hadn't paid attention to her. He hadn't taken any girl. He had saved himself for Sofia!

Sofia, he whispered, almost crying.

Your true love, Mabelline said. They say you want to build a bridge to her.

Yes.

I can't help you. I only have my flesh to give. I dreamed and yearned and prayed to Isis. Make me beautiful. My prayers were answered. I became a goddess of the flesh.

A transformation, Randy said.

Yes, but I lost something of the old me.

That's the way I feel! Randy exclaimed. I lived in the world of the gringos and lost part of who I really am! Or was! It's hard to explain.

Be careful what you wish for, Mabelline said sadly.

But you are beautiful, Randy said. Not just outside but inside. In your heart you have the beauty of Sofia.

Really?

Yes.

You're the first guy to ever say that.

I mean it.

Tears filled her eyes. I'm glad I ran into you, Ernie.

Randy.

Yes, Randy. Gosh, I wish I could remember— it doesn't matter. We both learned our lesson.

Yes, we have, Randy agreed.

Want to dance?

Not now. I have promises to keep.

You're a good man, Robby.

Ah— Randy said nothing.

I see some fellows waiting for me. She stood, then paused. Perhaps one is always losing part of one's self. You lived with the gringos and changed. Is that so bad?

I guess it's a kind of transformation, Randy answered. But sometimes I felt I didn't have a choice. Like I had to learn a new way of being. And deep inside it wasn't me.

That's the problem with communal life.

I see, Randy said. I was willing to learn. But I had to give up the language of my ancestors and my history. I felt I knew the Others but they really didn't know me.

Those in power write the history, she said. Well, tra-la-la. A fiesta's a fiesta, and all that. Más vale el baile que la iglesia.

The dance is better than church. Father Polonio wouldn't agree with that. Well, maybe sometimes.

Mabelline walked toward the swirling dust cloud the dancers had raised.

Nice costume! Randy shouted.

She turned and winked. This is real, silly. Then she disappeared.

Fourteen

Randy jumps into the River
of Life and nearly drowns.

Randy walked on. Oso briefly thought of following Cleopatra. She smelled like pepperoni pizza.

Sun-offf-a! he snuffed through his nose. Then casting a futile glance at the desert queen, he turned and followed his master.

After all, didn't the old man say that in a prior life Oso had been a Hapsburg prince? And princes are addicted to princesses. Oso could picture himself on a river barge with Mabelline.

Even though Agua Bendita was a small village, it seemed to Randy that every plausible character in the world had come to the fiesta. From Nero to the most recent dictators. Salesmen, brokers, artists, musicians, politicians, Rough Riders, knaves, Hollywood stars, Cossacks, on and on.

Where did they come from? Did the fiesta attract them, or was it all an illusion?

The business types were everywhere, hawking everything. The book *How to Make Money in Five Easy Lessons* was very popular, even though in Agua Bendita it was too late to make money.

Was everyone destined to continue buying and selling what they had bought and sold in time-past? Was this their penance? And did it mean they weren't moving up or down on the karmic scale? Stasis could be a definition of hell.

Movement and time go together. The old space-time thing. In the old myths time could be made to stand still. The underworld of the Greeks was caught in a time warp. Time crawled in Hades. The Greek heroes who fought at Troy just stood around bemoaning their fate. Was fate also an illusion? What was there to hold on to if one did not have a destiny?

Love? Yes, love could conquer time. Like when the Lover kissed the Beloved. A slurpy kiss could make time stand still. Everybody knew that. But was that also a lie? Love often moved on. Lovers parted or died. Nothing was permanent.

Was heaven also timeless? Did languid souls sit around caroling? Did the songs change? If there were only one song, the song-fest could drive a soul crazy.

Feeling confused and a bit let down, Randy sought solace at the river. He sat on the grassy bank, Oso curled up beside him. Dreaming dog dreams.

Across the river Sofia led her flock to the meadow. The lambs sprang up and down on wobbly legs, cavorting merrily. Butting heads and jumping over each other.

Just like us when we were kids, Randy thought.

Unica appeared. Hijo, you getting used to *here*?

Randy shook his head. I feel confused as ever, he replied.

Things change. Nothing is constant, not even here. People change. Saw you talking to Mabelline. Talk about change. She used to be a scrawny girl. Now every pendejo would like to pull her strings. Ring her bell. You know.

She is lovely.

But not as beautiful as Sofia, Unica said, looking across the river.

Why can't I just walk across? Randy cried in exasperation.

I told you! Only Jesus walks on water.

Will Sofia recognize me?

No sé, Unica replied. That's the big question. That's why you need to build your bridge. Every man has to do that. And every woman. But men are more easily distracted.

Is that what happened to me?

We are past judging the living or the dead. What happened happened. Ni modo. Time played its tricks on us. Now we are content to be here.

I'm not content! Randy cried. I should have known you can't go home again. Why is it so difficult? So painful?

Unica held his hand. Hijo, she whispered, the journey is never easy. We feel pain and suffer because we are earth people. Born of the earth, made of earth, we return to earth. The birth and death cycles of mother earth involve pain and suffering. Imagine the pain our mother feels when spring arrives. There's joy, but also terrible birth pangs. Winter closes in with its cold and freezes the skin of the earth. Darkness creates dread; earth's creatures suffer.

Should it be any different for us mortals, the clay people? The mysterious energies of mother earth awaken us. We feel awe and joy on the breast of the mother. But as the mother suffers pain, so do we. Asteroids deface the flesh of earth, continents groan and move, crashing painfully against each other, mountains topple, seas go dry, man poisons her— the mother suffers. Should it be any different for us, her children?

She paused. Tears wet her eyes.

Randy hung his head. I accept my suffering. If only I could reach Sofia. That's the only consolation I have left.

Unica fell silent. The poor boy was in pain. She had seen it before. A kind of angst. There was only one way to conquer it.

Wisdom is constant, she said. It's the seeker who frets. You need a purpose.

Build the bridge?

Yes. You're caught up in memory. Memories linger in the soul forever.

I thought even memories die.

When we get old, we think they die. They just get recycled. The universe is a memory. You are a man created in the image of God, the good book tells us. So you have God-thoughts.

Not God! But I'm not dumb! Randy cried. I went to night school! I read books! I wrote a book! I listened to classical music— Rachmaninoff! Tchaikovsky! Chuck Berry! I'm not stupid! But here I feel stupid! I feel it's all a game!

Oh my, Unica crooned. First denial, then rebellion. Like Lucifer. Our hero rebels on the bank of the River of Life. Is this a comedy or a tragedy?

What do you know? Randy cried. I read about a curandera far wiser than you! With that he jumped up and shouted to Sofia.

Sofia! It's me, Randy! Your true love!

He waved, and Sofia in all her glory took notice. She shaded her eyes and looked at the young man across the river.

She's waving at me!

No! Unica tried to hold him.

I'm coming! he called, and jumped into the river. Instantly the treacherous current swept him away like a piece of useless driftwood.

Unica shouted, Man overboard! Man overboard!

The tranquil mountain stream Randy thought he could wade across was indeed a raging torrent. Such is the River of Life, as many know. It's more than just a metaphor. It's for real.

The cold swirling water dragged Randy down into darkness. Huge foaming waves rose over him, and he could only flail his arms and try to stay afloat. For a moment he thought he saw the child whose name he bore. The angelic face floated before him. He reached out, but the child disappeared. Randy only went deeper into the vortex. Full fathom five.

¡Dios mío! he cried. He was drowning.

The River of Life is like that when one loses a job or loses faith, gets divorced, can't pay for the kid's braces, gets cancer or has a stroke, heart surgery, diabetes, drinks too much to forget a lost love, loses one's home, or the bank account evaporates. There are millions of depressions that stir the dark humours of the soul.

During the dark nights of the soul, life is barely worth living. Waves of despair suffocate both flesh and soul. No amount of thrashing or kicking or complaining will help. One only seems to sink deeper, just as Randy found himself sinking in the river.

But there is hope. Somehow the human spirit rebounds and finds a sliver of hope. No matter how far one sinks, the will to survive shines through. I can do it! the person cries. *¡Sí, se puede!* Randy thought. I will not be victim to circumstances!

Then the will to live raises the suffering soul out of its despair.

Gracias a Dios, some say in thanks. The humanists only pat themselves on the back.

Struggle! Struggle! It's all we know of life. That's the way it was ordained in the beginning.

Just as that thought crashed through his head, a wave of survival lifted Randy out of the watery depths to the heights.

From the crest of the wave, Randy now saw beautiful cumulus clouds rising over the mountain. Sunshine bathed the clouds; a rainbow arched across the valley. His sense of doom lifted for that moment.

I'm alive! Randy shouted.

Too soon! Those who have nearly drowned in the River of Life know the false feeling.

The next instant, watery fingers again pulled him down into

---

the deep. The River of Life doesn't play favorites. Or does it?

Sinking, swallowing water, exhausted, Randy remembered a note he had made: The rich *do* seem favored. They can buy expensive boats to navigate the river. They have all sorts of life jackets: bank accounts, brokers, and lawyers.

The poor have only leaky inner tubes.

The rich can buy mansions. They can afford insurance. They can send their kids to expensive private schools. No wonder the goal of so many is to be rich.

In the meantime, Oso ran along the bank barking, Help! Help! He also barked in Spanish in case the mexicanos were nearby. !Auxilio! !Auxilio!

He saw his master tossed about like a lost soul by the raging water. The current was so strong, Oso was afraid his master would not last. After all, who has ever outlasted the River of Life?

It so happened a fisherman on the bank heard Oso. He looked and saw a drowning Randy. Quickly he got in his skiff and rowed out into the foaming waters. Expertly he threw a lifeline, which Randy was able to grab.

Ahoy! he called. Neither the golden carp nor the white whale will claim you today!

It was obvious the paisano was not from the eastern seaboard, but he had read a book or two. And he had learned to navigate the river.

He pulled Randy aboard his skiff and skillfully rowed to shore. There he tossed a near-drowned Randy upon the blessed earth.

Gracias, Randy sputtered, coughing up dark water.

De nada, the paisano said. Glad to help.

Oso ran up and licked Randy's cold, wet face. You okay? You okay?

———

I'm okay, Oso. Thanks to this man.

Pedro, the man said. Got to get you dry. He took Randy's jacket, shirt, and pants, and laid them out near his campfire.

Be dry in no time, but I don't know about you. He chuckled. Life ain't easy. A valley of tears, as my poor mother used to say. Thank God we're *here*.

Fifteen

Pedro tells why he changed his name to Peter Rocks.

Pedro's campfire was the first warmth Randy had felt in Agua Bendita. If he didn't count the Devil's hot hands.

The sweet smoke from the juniper and piñón logs rose into the sky. The Día de Los Muertos clouds were now upside-down exclamation points. Like those in Spanish that tell the reader someone's about to shout or get emotional.

Randy's laptop didn't have upside-down exclamation marks, or if it did, he couldn't find them. Oh well, he would wing it. Use what he had, Chicano-style.

He thought ! looked better. The stem was erect. Upside-down, it looked like it was dripping. !Órale!

What would Quixote say about the strange happenings in the heavens?

Are the clouds an illusion? Randy asked. A dumb question.

Don't know, Pedro replied.

Does it ever rain here? he thought of asking. He still had the instincts of a farmer's son, the need to study rain clouds.

I'm Randy.

Bienvenido, Randy. I heard you came up the canyon and didn't look back. Good. But jumping in the river? That was dumb.

Randy agreed.

You sure must love Sofia.

I do.

You almost went full fathom five. One more fathom, and

who knows? At that depth your eyes become pearls. The fish eat the pearls, which become fish poo. You must've pissed off Poseidon.

I have cursed no gods, Randy replied.

Wait a minute, Pedro said thoughtfully. Then he's jealous! He doesn't want you to cross to Sofia! You're a hero, Randy!

I'm no hero. There are no Scylla and Charybdis *here*.

But La Llorona and El Coco live along the river. They eat young souls. And they do whatever Poseidon tells 'em.

Randy was in no mood to discuss old myths. Stories of water spirits and mermaids were a dime a dozen.

I'm just glad I didn't become fish poo, he said.

Me too, Pedro agreed. But nature recycles. When we were kids our parents told us the world was stable. There was heaven or hell. Angels or devils waiting for us. For others it's nirvana. That's what the Zen master tells me. But the universe is greedy. It doesn't like to lose a single iota of anything. You know.

Randy didn't know, but asked, Do things become better as we go through transformations? Do we gain wisdom? Of what use are we if we become fish droppings?

In the material world things just change form. But the soul absorbs beauty. Music, art, poetry, the beauty in nature, even our bodies are beautiful. We're creators of beauty. Unica tells us that's the purpose of life. Beauty and truth go on forever. Don't you think?

Yes, Randy said. Maybe that's why I came home.

That and Sofia, Pedro winked.

So you know.

The entire village knows. It's the love story of the day.

I was stupid to jump in.

Yeah, Pedro agreed. The River of Life isn't conquered in one day— though the young seem to think so.

I'm not young anymore, Randy said, looking up at the illusory clouds. I feel time pressing on me. How much time do I have?

Pedro shrugged. I don't know about time. It's just some dumb personal thing we used to worry about. Remember when we carried clocks strapped to our wrists? Doesn't mean a thing in the end.

What do you mean?

We can't measure time. Look around you. Even here everything is changing. You can't put your finger on it.

Randy looked. Yes even the here was changing to there and back again. The difference between *here* and *there* was a simple T. The cross? Was that it?

Come on, Pedro said. Let's eat. Nearly drowning makes a man hungry. Like after you make love to a beautiful woman. Or smoke a little pot. Good times call for munchies.

He took baked potatoes and a piece of charred bread from the coals and offered Randy the meal.

This is the first bread I've seen here, Randy said, biting into the hardtack. He felt a tooth crack.

Left over from the forty loaves, Pedro joked.

Any fish left over? Randy asked. He knew the Jesus story.

No, Pedro replied. It's a sin to eat the golden carp. Besides, all we have are potatoes.

You sit here all day and rescue drowning souls?

My destiny, Pedro answered. I know what it's like to be without purpose. In time-past I went from town to town, meal to meal. One day, bam! My heart said Agua Bendita was calling me back.

Did you come up the canyon? Randy asked.

Yes.

Saw the two-headed calf?

Yes. Everybody has to go by Todos Santos's place. Calls himself Gatekeeper.

I see. Did you by any chance know my father? Juan Diego. We lived just past Mabelline's home. Everybody knew him. A pomegranate tree grew in his front yard.

Pomegranate?

Yes. Beautiful little orange flowers in the spring. Made the old people dream of Spain. Then the red fruit in autumn. The kids stole the pomegranates.

Tart? Made your mouth wrinkle up?

Yes.

Pedro shook his head and chewed on the potato. The only father I know is up there. He pointed skyward.

Randy looked up. The sky was motionless. Idle as a stranded ship in the wide Sargasso Sea. Stale and gray. No horizon. The clouds had disappeared. An illusion. Just something he had wanted to see.

You from here? he asked.

Here's just a word, Randy. We're *here* and not *there*, then a second later *here* becomes *there*. The world is illusive. We try to make it exact, call it *here*. Now. But it moves too fast. Earth is moving across the Milky Way dragged by the sun. And the Milky Way is dragged by galactic forces. All headed toward the mother of all black holes. What choice do we have?

We have free will! Randy sputtered.

If you believe. What difference does it make?

I want to be master of my fate . . .

Pedro smiled. You must've gone to school.

Night classes, Randy said, not sure where the conversation

was going. Or what he really believed. Belief was not easy. It seemed to change as opportunities arose.

Have you forgotten everything? Randy asked.

Age does that. I feel two thousand years old. Besides, what's there to remember? Old stuff just makes you sad. Now I just sit here and fish.

Catch anything?

Caught you, didn't I? Pedro laughed and threw Oso a piece of bread, which the small dog chewed like an old bone.

Randy was intrigued by the fisherman who caught those drowning in the River of Life.

And your family?

My family was from the village of Peñasco. We were known as los Peñascos. My father was a strict penitente, so I left home soon as I could. Joined an evangelist. In the old days they used to go from village to village, set up a tent and chairs, and preach salvation. Now they have fancy glass churches and television shows. Making money.

Who was the evangelist? Randy asked.

Some hippie. Nice guy. Really believed in helping the poor. A few of us wandered around with him. One day we found ourselves in a very conservative town. The officials threw our leader in jail.

Officials?

Yeah. The government didn't like his message of peace. The military complex can't get Fed money if there's peace.

What happened to him?

Crucified, I guess. I took off. I knew I had to learn English if I was going to survive in Anglolandia.

Randy's ears perked up. So you know what it's like!

Oh, yes. I was a poor kid with a funny name. Pedro Peñasco. The Anglos couldn't pronounce Peñasco so they called me

Pee-dro Pecker. I changed my name. I became Peter Rocks. You know peñasco means a big rock. From then on I got respect.

You assimilated?

Pedro nodded. Sooner or later they make gringos of us all. Even the saints are white in the movies and in the Christmas cards. As if Jesus came from Norway. Only la Virgen de Guadalupe stayed brown. And even she is white in some of those statues made in Ohio.

Randy nodded. He knew. You like it here?

How much choice do we really have? Is there fate? Destiny? Is our life preordained? If I hadn't been exactly here at this time and place, would you have drowned? Lost your soul forever.

We do have choices, Randy said lamely.

Pedro shrugged. You've been among the gringos too long. Choice drives their economy. Choice is good. The more the better. You ever buy breakfast cereal or soap or a TV set? Hundreds to choose from! Drives people bipolar. But they say choice creates competition. Like the Devil told you, mejor el baile que la iglesia. More choices at the dances than at church. He laughed.

But I have free will! Randy insisted.

You believe that? The Dance of Life and the River of Life. Prove to me where you find free will in the fast-moving *there* to *here*.

Randy had no proof. The world had no proof. It was full of conundrums. Like, could God make a stone so big he couldn't lift it? Which came first, the chicken or the egg? How many angels can sit on the head of a pin? Childish stuff.

He thought that Agua Bendita would have answers. It didn't work that way.

What do I do? Randy asked.

Build your bridge, Pedro replied.

Then I'll know!

A used car salesman would give you a guarantee. You can't get one here.

They heard anguished voices in the mist.

What's that?

Young souls drowning, Pedro said. I gotta go!

He jumped into his skiff and disappeared in the fog that rose like a curtain over the foaming waters.

Randy could hear cries for help. So many young souls drowning in the River of Life.

Sixteen

Randy meets a variety of characters at La Fiesta.

Randy put on his pants and shirt and walked up the river. He shivered. His jacket was too wet to wear, so he hung it on a tree. It was the jacket his father had given him when he left home and he hated to leave it behind.

His grandfather had worn it when he went to Wyoming to shepherd sheep. Other times he went to Colorado to work in the potato harvest. The people of Agua Bendita went far and wide to work, but they always returned home. That's how it had been for centuries.

La patria chica. Each village, our little country. Sacred earth. Polis. Like the Greek city-states.

The hispano villages didn't produce an Aeschylus, but they had drama. The sacred dance of los Matachines performed to the lilting tune of fiddle and guitar while two rows of masked figures danced. The little girl dressed in first-communion white was the Virgin Mary; for the ancient mexicanos she was Malinche. She danced for the Monarca, Moctezuma, and led him out of the Aztec underworld to lead the twelve tribes again.

The time of the mestizo was at hand.

A boy acted the part of the Bull. Playful, charging the kids in the crowd, but also representing the dark side of the human soul. El Toro had to be controlled by the mayordomos and led away. Thus the ancient struggle between good and evil was portrayed for grateful audiences.

Then resurrection! Promise! Return! The Virgin led the Monarca back to his people! He would lead the twelve tribes against all enemies. Or as some would have it, he entered the church and became a good Christian. Indians watching the drama got the message.

In the village of Talpa, descendents of Comanches danced in celebration of their roots. Comanche progeny, whose ancestors had generations ago been taken prisoner by the nuevo mexicanos. They became Hispanicized, but they didn't forget their roots. Whooping village boys danced in Comanche regalia. The battles that brought those Plains Indians to live with the españoles-mexicanos of the Río Grande Valley were acted out. They remembered.

The first españoles-mexicanos who arrived in New Mexico had presented various plays. On horseback and with much drama, *Los Moros y los Cristianos* was a favorite. The Pueblo people looked on as the Moorish sultan surrendered to the Catholic knights. The message to the natives was clear. Come into the church.

Ah, the Pueblo people ahhed. That Jesucristo is a pretty strong guy. Best pay attention.

So much proselytizing.

Las Pastorelas of Christmas reenacted the journey of shepherds on their way to the birth of Jesus. In *Las Posadas*, San José and the Virgin Mary sought shelter until they found a welcoming home, the church.

Plenty of communal drama. And always the chorus of village elders telling stories, telling and retelling the children the stories of the eternal battle between good and evil.

The tragedies had not produced a grand tragic figure. No Oedipus, Quixote, Hamlet, not even a Pedro Páramo. There did exist in the folk tales the comic pícaro, Pedro de Ordimalas. Hollywood had not yet discovered him. Probably never would.

So, the dramas remained communal. The community, like the family, was bonded together in prayer and survival. Without the bond of community, survival was tenuous. No player dared step out of the chorus and tell his tragic story. That would come later.

Now the traditional culture of the ancestors was dying. Death of the traditional culture meant the children would lose their attachment to the land. The spiritual teachings of the ancestors would wither.

Everyone was into becoming gringos.

What did you find? Randy asked Oso. A turtle stood in their path. Oso sniffed and got a squirt of turtle pee.

Caa-bro-naaa, he growled, wiping his nose.

Randy laughed. I nearly drowned, but the turtle continues on its path. Así es.

Colorful ducks honked, circled, and landed softly in the river, hardly rippling the water.

A red fox ran into a thicket. Blackbirds with orange-tipped wings landed on swaying reeds. Green lizards scurried to find holes for hibernating. Goldfish swam languidly in the nearby pond. Suspended in the dark water.

A season of hibernation. Everything going to sleep.

A season of darkness had come over the valley. A season of rest. Green branches gone dormant. All going underground.

The sun was setting on the Western Isles.

Drugstore cowboys drank potato whiskey, sang sad songs, and got in fights. Not a good sign. Doom prevailed. The empire was sinking. The money-changers clutched at green bucks, as if money were the raft that would keep them afloat.

I have to hurry and build the bridge, thought Randy.

The River of Life thrashed and twisted like an angry serpent.

Overhead, long Vs of honking geese and sand cranes. Etched against the sky, hardly moving, heading nowhere. The season was deep into rest.

With his tongue Randy felt the pomegranate seed stuck between his teeth.

I ate a pomegranate the day I left home, he remembered.

Across the river Sofia drove her lambs to the meadow, where they would nibble on dry clumps of sweetgrass. She would sit under her father's cherry tree, card wool, fall asleep.

An angel would descend with a youthful dream for Sofia. In her dream the boys from the village came to pick cherries. Each thought he could win Sofia's favor. There was only one she would have. That was the boy named for three saints whose names nobody could remember.

She would moan in her sleep. The gushing river would conjure images of pleasure domes. That was the nature of true love.

Randy approached the fiesta. It was a bit warmer now. The music, the Ferris wheel, and the merry-go-round had stopped. The booths where potato fries and potato pancakes had been sold now stood sullen. Vendors dozed.

La Muerte and the Devil sat conversing.

Hey kid, the Devil called. You look a little wet!

Maybe he doesn't swim too good, Death chortled. Wet behind the ears!

They fell to laughing at Randy's expense.

Mejor el baile que la iglesia, they said in unison.

What baile? Randy asked.

El Baile de los Muertos. Esta noche.

Dance of the Dead. Tonight. Everyone is going home to dress for the dance. You coming?

Maybe he doesn't have a date!

They laughed again.

I don't have time for dancing, Randy replied, irritated.

Why had the surroundings changed? Why in a land that had no clocks was he feeling the pressure of time?

Under a dead cottonwood sat Mabelline. She looked forlorn. Her mascara had run. Her Egyptian crown tilted sideways. Cleopatra had aged.

Mabelline?

Sad eyes looked up. Hi, Tomás.

Randy.

Oh, hi, Randy. You going to the dance?

Randy shook his head and moved on. A sense of dread returned. He had thought his hometown would be a place of joy. He remembered how close neighbors had been when he was a child. Now everything seemed topsy-turvy.

Was he doing penance like the book lady? Were they all doing penance? For what? And why the costumes?

The thought struck like a jolt of electricity. Was he too in costume? Was this not the Randy he knew, but another Randy? Someone from another time?

He rushed to the river and looked into the still water. He touched his face, looked into his eyes. It was him, but changed. How? And could he trust the reflection in the River of Life? He knew it could be deceiving.

Why me? he moaned. Why? All I wanted was to live a normal life. Be like the guy next door. Joe Smith. Yes, if I could have it all back I would even be a gringo!

Randy shouted at the sky. They're not bad! They just have

different ways! They're a cultural group! Like other groups! We got to respect each other! We got to get along!

We wholeheartedly agree with you, young man, said the voices.

Randy turned. Two men. The one in the tattered frock coat was a judge. The one holding out his hand was a politician.

Around them everything was falling into dust, rotting, the creaking Ferris wheel rusting. The colorful streamers blowing away in a gusting wind.

Judge?

Yes, son.

Is there justice in the world?

The judge cleared his throat. I can only administer the law, not write it. He turned to the politician.

The man's eyelids fluttered. A sure sign of a man about to tell a lie. We try to write laws that are fair. Equality and all that.

But there is no equality, Randy protested. People are either top, middle, or the lowly poor. The top group has more equality, that's obvious.

Somebody has to run the world, the judge said. Equality doesn't mean you can be like the next guy. It's only an abstract goal.

This young man is obviously a malcontent, the politician said, withdrawing his hand.

Abstract goal? Randy repeated.

Of course. Did you really expect to find equality? the judge asked.

Yes!

Ah, that's your problem. You should just try to get along. Live and let live. Go with the flow. Don't rock the boat.

Let sleeping dogs lie, the politician added. Don't cry over

spilt milk. Nobody ever promised you a rose garden—

Stop! Randy shouted. Equality, fraternity, liberty! All abstractions? Don't you believe in them?

Of course, the politician said. That's how we earn our money.

Long live equality, fraternity, life, liberty, and the pursuit of happiness! the judge shouted. We know our Constitutional rights!

But the rich get richer and the poor poorer! Randy protested.

That's progress. Special interests and lobbyists foot the bill. Grease the wheel. You scratch my back—

Don't bite the hand that feeds you, the politician said. Who are we to place regulations on ambition?

But when ambition becomes greed—

Poor boy, the judge said. You've got it all wrong. Greed becomes ambition. Greed is the oil that lubricates industry!

The way it should be, his friend said, and they teetered away. It was obvious they had drunk too much fermented potato beer.

Randy shook his head. Is everyone going mad or just me?

Ah, don't believe those two old fools, Unica said. She drew Randy to a wood bench under a pomegranate tree.

Who are they? Randy asked.

Characters, she replied. They come to the fiesta. Look! There's a general with his defense department. A doctor with his prescriptions. A teacher with books. A carpenter with tools. Attorneys with law books. A plumber, a Wall Street broker, pilot, nurse, television and movie stars, on and on. There is no end to the characters represented here.

Randy looked. The line of characters seemed to stretch to infinity.

They come to do business, Unica said. The business of business is business. Make! Make! Make! The more you make the more you sell. All to gain a penny from the next pendejo! And the next penny might break the camel's back.

It's happened before, Randy said.

Comes in cycles, Unica agreed. Every one of these characters has a story to tell. But you don't have to listen. You would be here forever.

Isn't *here* forever?

Ahem, Unica cleared her throat. She didn't want to give him a clue.

I feel lost. What must I do? Randy asked.

Stick to your purpose. Build your bridge.

To Sofia! To another world! What's on the other side?

Don't know, Unica replied.

Don't know! It's the only thing I have to do, and I don't know where it will get me! Will Sofia recognize me?

Unica scratched her scalp. Her hair had grown thin from scratching when she counseled the young. Her body was bent with the weight of the questions they asked. It was much easier to search for herbs than advise the young.

Hijo, she said, the soul goes on transforming itself. This you've been told. If Sofia recognizes you is up to you.

Seventeen

Unica points at the house with the pomegranate tree.

The pomegranate tree looked like a shabby Christmas tree. Prior seasons of dry, wrinkled fruit clung to its branches. It would look pretty if snow covered it.

Randy remembered eating one of the juicy fruits the day he left Agua Bendita. His mother blessed him. His father looked forlorn. Their only son was leaving home. A season would end; a new one waited on the horizon.

This is the house of my father! Randy said, suddenly surprised. I've been looking for it! How did you know?

Everyone knows the legend of the pomegranate tree, Unica replied.

There's a legend?

A simple story. He who eats a pomegranate will return the following season.

Randy remembered. There was a Greek myth. Who? A girl kept by Hades in the underworld. Persephone. Would she return to Agua Bendita? Ever?

My father kept the tree alive by covering it with straw in winter. It never froze, and every spring it flowered.

That's the lesson life teaches: seed, flower, fruit. Within the fruit, the seed again. Cycles the earth nurtures. The stories of eternal return are grounded in nature.

Unica spoke mythology.

She paused, then said, All life is grounded in nature.

And the spirit? Randy asked.

It, too, flows from nature. If we include the universe and its mystery. Galaxies of souls out there, all being recycled. Our mother recycles everything.

Mother?

God.

I see, he said, but he didn't. She called God the mother. And the universe a mystery. And the Mystery was God. What did Unica mean?

The seed needs to fall on fertile ground, my father taught me.

True enough, Unica agreed. But even a mountain of iron will be worn down by rain, wind, and sun. The wind deposits seeds in the smallest niche. Sprouts will take root and iron becomes a forest. Life wears death down.

Life wears death down, he repeated. He didn't know.

A truth of faith, she said.

And iron becomes trees, thought Randy. Her faith is strong. I have much to learn.

He looked at the dilapidated adobe home. The front door hung from only one hinge. The windows were broken, the blue paint cracked and faded.

I used to dream of this place. I imagined my parents sitting under the tree. On summer afternoons they sat in the shade. Father worked all day in the fields. Perhaps I should have been a farmer and stayed home.

A sadness crept into his heart. What had he gained by living among the gringos? What had he lost?

His view of the world had expanded. That was true. So many said it was the time of the gringo. Everybody was becoming gringos. But would natural cycles change even their time?

He knew it would have been the same if he had lived in any

other culture. If he had lived with Buddhists, he would have become one. If in France, he would speak French. He could be Jewish or Hindu. On and on.

Humans put on the coat of the culture and environment in which they live. One could wear many coats. The trick was to keep true to the original culture, the way of the ancestors.

But the spirit! Yes! The soul would not disappear. The soul was universal. The soul was constant!

The purpose of living was to expand the soul. Make it big as the universe. The original seed, the soul, had been deposited by the ancestors. It would flower, become fruit within the body, and return to seed.

Cycles. The universal soul was the original seed, coming into being with the big bang.

Ah, what did he know?

If one was lucky, one would eventually find the humanity of the soul. But few did.

Randy sighed.

What if I had not taken the open road that day? The Road of Life. Who would I be? Where?

No way to know, Unica said. What's preordained is preordained.

Do you believe that?

When it suits me, she replied. We often bend philosophy and religion to suit our needs.

Are there no absolute truths?

This is it, she said. What you see is what you get.

Randy sighed. He had found his father's house, but what good did that do?

He looked around. Nothing seemed the same.

All things change, Unica said. Summer becomes fall, autumn turns into winter, then spring, on and on. The seasons weather everything down.

The moon abides, Randy said, imagining some stability he could trust. Farmers trust the moon's cycles!

Even the moon will one day fall, the sun go blind.

Randy shivered. Angelica had told him the greatest fear of mankind was that of eternal darkness.

Will the sun really disappear? he asked.

In time. Nothing is permanent. Galaxies disappear into other universes. Hard to know what's out in the Great Mystery. We can count the stars and predict their birth. So what. All we know is we came from *there* to *here*. The cycles roll along like the wheels on Doña Sebastiana's cart.

She was La Comadre, a skeleton carrying a bow and arrow. The arrow of death. The penitentes said she rode a carreta, an old nuevo mexicano wood cart.

Had the train run into her on the way to Santa Fe?

What can I cling to? Randy cried.

Beauty and truth, Unica replied.

The beauty of Sofia?

Yes.

Do the angels or the Devil play a role in this?

Angels appear in dreams. They are messengers. The Devil knows more than we give him credit for knowing. After all, he's as old as fire. So they say. Beauty and truth are all we need. Create beauty in your soul and it will shine with truth. The form and the ideal reflect each other. Beauty and truth become the spirit of new beginnings.

Create beauty, Randy whispered.

Be kind to others is the only rule I know. Couple kindness with good deeds. Then the soul will shine with beauty and radiate out truth. Everything we do should partake in the beautiful. From that flows truth.

———

She winked. Or the other way around.

A teacher told me to nurture my imagination.

The creative imagination *is* the soul, Unica said.

My imagination is my soul?

As long as you keep it active and growing. Keep the faith.

I had faith when I was a child.

Faith springs eternal.

Maybe I forgot, Randy whispered. My teacher said in the end gold and possessions are worthless.

A wise woman, Unica nodded.

I began to read. Poetry, stories, everything I could find. I walked in nature. The trees spoke. Insects, animals, everything came alive.

You filled your soul with beauty.

Yes. But not enough, Randy moaned. I was foolish. I wasted my time. Now I feel it's too late.

Too late! Too late! Unica exclaimed. It's too late if you sit on your ass! There is work yet to be done, a purpose to challenge you!

The bridge!

Yes! You may find bliss in building the bridge. Find the grace that fills the universe. The simplest task must harmonize with the symphony of life. But beware. Work can be a double-edged sword. It can liberate or be the drudgery that enslaves the soul. Choose wisely.

The bridge, Randy repeated. Maybe it's not too late. What would my father say?

He's there, Unica pointed.

A surprised Randy stood.

Our home?

Así es.

He walked into the house. His mother stood at the stove, frying potatoes that sputtered in a skillet.

As it used to be, Randy marveled. A sense of awe flowed through him.

A pot of beans bubbled on the stove, the aroma filling the kitchen. She had baked a pile of mouth-watering tortillas. Green chile flavored with meat excited trickles of saliva in Randy's mouth. Chopped calabacitas with fresh corn simmered in cream.

My favorite meal! he exclaimed. He reached out to touch his mother.

Mamá, he said, but she did not turn.

At the table sipping a cup of coffee sat his father.

Papá, he said. He wanted to hug the old man as he used to when he was a child.

They were talking.

I miss mi'jito, she said. It has been a long time.

His father laughed. There is no time in Agua Bendita. One minute is like the next. He had to go see the world.

Yes. He had to learn how the Others live.

He will be hungry when he returns.

Bendito sea Dios, his father said.

Randy realized they had been here all along. His mother's kitchen was heaven. That's what he'd felt as a child. Heaven was his mother's kitchen!

Neighbors visited. Kind people who all their lives had done good deeds. Randy felt comforted.

Gracias, he whispered.

They had spoiled him. He was their only son. But they had taught him the values of Unica. Be kind to others, do good deeds.

Beauty flowed from those values and the village lived in harmony. Life was difficult, but the goodness of neighbors made it take on a deeper, wiser meaning. That was the way of his ancestors.

But nothing lasts forever. The cycles rolled on. How could they hold on to that beauty that gave a satisfying meaning to life?

Your faith is strong, his father said when they parted. Take our values with you wherever you go. Be kind to others and do good deeds.

Sí, Papá, Randy said. Gracias.

He walked out of the simple home as he had years ago.

Nothing is lost, he said to Unica.

True, she replied.

I should get to work.

Atta boy! Unica shouted. She jumped up and hugged the young man who was named for three saints whose names nobody could remember.

By the way, Randy said, who really destroyed the bridge? Was it the angel Espantoso as you said?

Unica looked embarassed. No.

But you said—

You know there are many versions.

Yes. So who was it?

Sofia.

Sofia? Why?

With no bridge to build you would be stuck here. You would not have a purpose. We have to keep moving. It's a law of nature.

I can't do it alone.

What are neighbors for? There's help. And the mejicanos

will help. They came to work, but they can't cross the river until a bridge is built.

I'll ask for help. !Sí, se puede!

!Sii-se-puede! Oso barked joyously, sensing his master's renewed confidence

Eighteen

Randy reads *How to Build a Bridge* and meets the *mexicano* workers.

Randy sat by the river and opened *How to Build a Bridge*. Subtitle: *Five Easy Lessons*.

Randy smiled. His night-school teacher had encouraged the class to write how to books. Recover from cancer, manage diabetes, lose weight, become a millionaire, touch your inner child— you name it. All could be solved in how to books.

The charlatans advertising on television sold such books twenty-four hours a day.

The public no longer reads literature, the teacher told the students. They prefer how to books. Or books for dummies. Movie stars and politicians who get in trouble write their stories overnight and make millions. They hire ghost writers. There's more money in writing these instant books than serious literature. Why can't you?

Randy knew gringos read how to books. These books perfected resolving the conflicts and traumas of life in five easy lessons. Wow! If that were true, gringo culture would last forever. Was it that simple?

I should try it, Randy said to Oso. Maybe I should title my book *How to Live Among the Gringos*. Put how to on the title to grab the reader's attention.

The answer was simple: assimilate. Gringo society insisted on homogeneity. Forget the ways of your ancestors. Forget your language and history. It's the American way.

Randy groaned. Did I become a gringo? He made a note:

My intention was not to be negative when I wrote the book. I didn't want to put down the gringos. It's too easy to fear and hate those who are not like us. It's too easy to make scapegoats of the Others.

But that's what the world keeps doing.

I wrote the book to show how different cultures affect each other. The good and not-so-good. Gringos, like any other group, are just different. That's all.

Living with them, I became like them. And as I became more and more like them, I felt I had lost something of the old me. So how did living in another culture affect me? Why do I feel I lost part of who I am?

Who was I? Who am I now?

Did the transformative powers of the universe bring me to Agua Bendita to recover my true self? The real me?

People and place form the man, and that inheritance nurtures the soul.

Where is my soul? What does it look like?

Listen, Oso. Randy read the *How to Build a Bridge* introduction: Life is like a river. It takes will power to succeed. You need the right attitude! Get aggressive or get out! Build your bridge or the currents of life will toss you like driftwood! Use your will power! It's up to you!

Oso placed his paws over his ears.

I know, I know, Randy said. Clichés. Life is like a river isn't used anymore.

The writers in the classes he had taken used metaphors like life is a wireless message. Or life is like a wormhole; welcome to a new dimension. Or life is the World Wide Web; be the spider.

Randy turned the page. The book preached self-reliance, rugged individualism, my way or the highway. Same message he had seen in movies as a kid. One man led the westward movement. He cleared out the natives and killed the buffalo. Why did the gringos make him a hero? Cause he had done it in five easy lessons, that's why.

Bullshit, Randy whispered, but continued reading.

Lesson one: Where There's a Will, There's a Way.

Will power seemed to be something one could buy at Walmart. Those with rich fathers could buy more.

Lesson two: Test the Waters.

Millions tested the waters daily and drowned. No education, no job, no hope. And no rich father.

Lesson three: The Strong Currents of Life Can Be Navigated!

Ten percent of the population owns speedboats and yachts. The other ninety percent have inner tubes with holes in them.

Randy paused and made a note: Something wrong with this picture.

Lesson four: Be Competitive!

This's it! The supreme value! Competition! Knock the other guy down and get ahead! Drive out the competitor! Save the Christian ethic for Sunday mornings. Those in power believed cooperation was communism, to be despised.

How sad, he thought. Ah well, let's plow ahead.

Lesson five: You're Ready! So Go Get It! Don't Let Anyone Stand in Your Way!

He closed the book. How sad. According to the author, getting ahead was like building a bridge, and all could be summed up in Five Easy Lessons.

But what of emotions? Heartbreak. Grief. Depression. Getting old. The death of a child or a partner. Fear of flying or global warming. Hemorrhoids. Not to worry, there were books on how to treat everything.

What do you think, Oso?

Burrr-shut! Oso barked, and ran off to chase butterflies.

Randy studied the bountiful face of the mountain. Along the river grew cottonwoods, river willows, elms, Russian olives. Up the slope of the hill grew junipers and wise old piñón trees. Piñón nuts were like money in the bank for the natives. A cash crop.

During childhood winters Randy often sat with his grandfather in front of the wood-burning stove, listening to abuelo's stories and eating piñón nuts. His abuelo told cuento after cuento. A treasure of folk tales brought by the españoles-mexicanos to New Mexico. Story time. The stories eroded present tense and warped into a timeless tense.

Ah, he sighed. As it used to be. We lived in paradise and didn't know it.

Higher up the mountain grew the stately ponderosa pines, groves of aspen, fir, blue spruce.

Up there flew eagles, vultures, playful black ravens, blue jays, owls. In the valley flew the lowly sparrows, magpies, and blackbirds with spots of orange on their wings. Quail. Playful roadrunners. Magical hummingbirds.

The strata on the face of the mountain told the history of the earth.

Best trust in nature, Randy thought. He whistled for Oso and started up the Mountain of the Singing Trees.

The higher he climbed the more symphonic the music. The mantra of the tall, swaying pines was complemented by the dainty, shivering aspen. The mountain breeze conducted, and the forest animals lent their melodious calls.

At the foot of a pine tree Randy spotted something shiny in a dry pile of bear scat. He kicked the pile and exposed a silver belt buckle. Rodeo Champion, Laramie, Wyoming. The buckle he had seen on the old man.

———

A few feet away the entire frame of a horse. It had been picked clean by insects. The rib cage, vertebrae, and large leg bones shone calcium-white. Washed by rain and bleached by the sun, the skeleton would in time dissolve into the earth.

That is if some crazy artist didn't pick up the hip bones and take them to her studio.

Spirit the horse had remained loyal to his master.

A startled Randy moved away. He peered into the dark forest. Forest creatures were watching him. In a grove of quivering aspen, people moved.

!Buenos días! Randy called.

!Amigo! a man called back.

Randy and Oso wandered over to the camp. Mexican workers headed north had paused to rest.

!Jesús Malverde! the man shouted and hugged Randy. !Ay, qué gusto!

!Jesús Malverde! the workers cried, and gathered around Randy, touching him and whispering, Gracias a Dios. They thought the Mexican Robin Hood had arrived to help them.

The deceased Malverde was a hero of poor mexicanos, but recently he had become the patron saint of the narcotraficantes. The drug cartels also prayed to the saints.

Randy blushed. No. No soy Malverde. Soy Randy.

Ran-dee?

Sí, Randy.

Oh. The man looked disappointed.

!No es Malverde! he said, and his words went trembling among the workers. The women sighed. The men shook their heads.

Qué lástima, the man said. Come sit down. He pointed to a tree stump near the campfire. We keep fire small. Don want la migra to see us.?Tienes hambre?

Randy politely said no but nevertheless a woman offered him a raw potato and water.

You are no mejicano, the man said.

I was born here, Randy replied. My parents also.

Oh. ?Un pocho?

No.

?Chicano?

Sí.

Es Chicano, he smiled and informed his fellow workers. Ah, they nodded their approval.

What you do?

I came to cut trees.

Why for?

To build a bridge.

Ay, carajo. ?Pa' qué?

To cross the river.

Quiere llevantar un puente, the man said, and the crowd of workers whispered, ?Un puente?

Why for?

Maybe he has a novia there, the woman who had given him the potato suggested.

She knows, Randy thought. Woman's intuition.

A girl friend, the man said. Qué bueno. But you need papers to build a bridge. In this country you need papers even to fart.

The workers laughed.

I don't need no stinking papers! Randy replied.

His reply surprised even him. Had reading the *How to Build a Bridge* book made him aggressive? Was this a will to power he was feeling, or simply gas from the raw potato?

The mexicanos liked his bravado. They smiled and drew near.

!Órale! they said. He don need no stinken papers!

But why?

Sofia of the Lambs lives on the other side of the river, Randy said.

Ahh, the handsome woman said. I tol you. Mi'jito has a girl. Not just any girl, compadres. Muy especial. All these years Sofia has remained a virgin.

Ahhh, the workers said, and nodded. A virgin. That was worth a bridge.

I need help, Randy said, looking up at the stately pines.

Seguro que sí. How much you pay?

I have no money.

Ahhh. A Chicano without money. So often the case.

Okay, okay, the man said. For love we don take money. My name is José. I am a carpenter. I have a saw, hammer, nails. I will help.

We will help, the woman said. My name is María.

Okay Randee. We help. To build a bridge por amor es un honor.

The people cheered and picked up their tools. !Seguro que sí! To build a bridge for love was an honor!

Unica appeared. The workers greeted her with respect. La curandera, they whispered.

Randy hugged her. You were right! The workers will help!

Así es, Unica smiled. But before you cut the trees you need their permission.

Sí, por supuesto, the workers nodded.

She knelt at the trunk of a tree. Hermanos y hermanas, we ask permission to take you from the earth. In your new life you will be a Bridge of Love.

Qué milagro, the workers smiled and whispered. Un puente de amor.

They understood life was a series of transformations. You sweat and work hard all your life, and for what? For *nada*! At the end there is *nada*. Maybe your familia cries over the coffin. That's all.

But if you could be part of a beautiful transformation, like making green trees into a Bridge of Love— then life had meaning.

The pine trees swayed in the wind and assented. The song of the trees joined the song of the river. The tired feet of workers would cross the river on planks hewn from stately pines.

!A trabajar! José called.

We don need no stinken papers! someone shouted. The workers picked up the refrain, which went echoing down the mountainside.

We don need no stinken papers!

In the dark, ghost-filled cantina, a breeze swayed the cobwebs hanging from the ceiling. A rattler silently swished across the floor. Mice scurried.

Squat turned to Bob. By god, I think those Mexicans are gonna do it!

Nineteen

The mob rebels against the bridge-building. Todospedo the mayor makes Randy an offer he can't refuse.

Sap flows and buds erupt. Blossoms bloom and are kissed by bees, dark-winged moths, and long-tongued hummingbirds. Flower becomes fruit. After a season the fruit drops to earth.

Earth dissolves the fruit-shell, exposing the seed. Atavistic genetic codes awaken in the seed germ and send out dull white roots and yellow-green tendrils. A squashy thing of no beauty to the untrained eye, but in each sprig sleeps one of these beautiful pine trees.

Unica was musing.

Sunlight! I seek sunlight! the living cells cry. This is the Passion of Nature.

The Passion of Nature, Randy whispered. What does it mean?

Our mother earth is a passionate mother, Unica replied. Aren't all females? She winked.

The mexicana women understood. Wives of farmers, they knew the earth as a warm womb that gave forth her fruit. Like a woman's womb produced children. They also knew passion required work.

I thought only humans— Randy stopped. Best to listen.

Mother nature's passion is pure love. She gives and asks nothing in return. The sun, the stars, and all galaxies run on passion.

Gracias a Dios they don't run on oil, someone whispered.

Randy was puzzled. He knew how his father and neighboring farmers had worked and loved the earth. But galaxies in the farthest reaches of cold space? What did all that dark matter know of passion?

I don't get it.

God is passion. Coming into being requires the heat of passion. A big bang, some say. Tata Dios y Mamá Dios created a hot fire. The universe and our earth were born of that Love. We humans try to imitate.

The workers nodded. It was true. Man struggled to be like the great powers above and below. But he remained a mere spark compared to the original burst of passion.

How long does it take to learn this simple truth? Randy asked.

When you love, you feel true passion in your heart. Love is creativity. It never ends. Everything in nature keeps changing and evolving. Transformation is fueled by passion.

Does it ever stop?

Oh no, hijito, it never stops.

Is there a divine plan?

Of course. Tata Dios y Mamá Dios are the universe. Mamá Dios dresses in a skirt of stars. Like the Milky Way. Es muy bonita. Hand in hand the two play hopscotch.

Así es, the workers smiled. They had paused to listen. They prayed to Tata Dios, but who was Mamá Dios?

Is she la Virgen de Guadalupe? a woman asked.

Or some ancient Aztec goddess?

The goddesses are manifestations of the feminine universe. As are all females. The big bang was created by male and female energies. It takes two to tango. She winked.

And us? Randy asked.

Each person is a galaxy.

———

Me a galaxy? Awesome!

Your soul is a galaxy. Within the soul lies an astrolabe, a compass like the one Ulysseus used to cross the wine-dark sea. The soul sails across the greater universe, seeking unity with the Universal Soul. Your compass guides you to Sofia.

Yes, Randy said. The inner compass in his soul led him to Sofia. It could not be otherwise.

Where did you learn this?

I didn't go to night school but I read a few books, Unica replied. The mexicanos laughed. She was a wise woman born of the earth. She had studied the map of the heavens by living rooted in nature.

I thought the answer was up there, Randy pointed at the immense bowl of sky.

You do your work on earth, let the up there take care of itself.

Así es. The workers nodded and went back to cutting pine trees for the bridge.

No man knows the ways of God. Man is a blind creature struggling in the vast world of illusions. Best trust your inner light. That's the compass.

Randy nodded. He knew about illusions. Anything that occurred in time had to be illusion, since time itself was such.

Meanwhile, back in the village, the rumor had spread that the mexicanos were building a bridge. This upset the movers and shakers of Agua Bendita.

Some of the youngsters in the village had joined the effort, picking up axes and tools and heading up the mountain.

The movers and shakers accused the bridge-builders of high treason. A mob gathered to listen.

A man named Vendo protested the loudest. If tree-cutting continues, there won't be a Dance of the Dead tonight! It's his fault— the young man named after three saints whose names no one remembers!

The mob trembled with fear. In the history before histories, the Dance of the Dead had never been cancelled.

He calls himself Randy, Vendo's partner Compro piped up. We have to stop him! We don wanna know what's on the other side!

We don wanna know! the mob cried.

To know is forbidden!

We're happy in our ignorance!

He ruins the young. Some are helping him. They want to cross the river! They want to know! We will lose them!

Horrors! Treason! Blasphemy! Apostate!

Some shouted, Communist! The old bugaboo word most used by the fear-mongers.

What *is* on the other side? an innocent child asked.

Unica answered, Sofia of the Lambs lives there. She who embodies true wisdom. When you open your hearts and minds to Sofia you will know beauty and truth.

Wisdom! Vendo protested. There's only one wisdom: buy and sell!

The mob clamored in agreement, Buy and sell!

The man who sold potato vodka shouted above the rest. We've invested too much in the Dance of the Dead to cancel even one night! It's been tried before and the world suffered for it!

Not even Jesus can cancel the dance! another added.

What the hell are we gonna do?

A rabid man cried, I say we send the Mexicans back where they came from! Declare them illegal!

Unica held up her hand. No human is illegal on this earth. We are all equal in God's eyes.

Our country, right or wrong! a woman shouted.

Boundaries that separate nations are created by men, Unica answered. Jesus will come to erase all borders.

Trouble-maker! Vendo shouted. We don need you!

Go join the other trouble-makers!

Their curses drove Unica away.

Listen, Compro said. I say we arrest this Randy. He needs a permit to build a bridge!

He needs a permit! the malcontents shouted through spittle as corrosive as acid. Grab Randy! No permit, no bridge!

Viva the Dance of the Dead!

!Vivan los muertos! they shouted.

Wait! How do we trap Randy?

Send the Devil!

!Sí! !El Demónio!

Compro raised his hand. Wait! Randy knows the Devil lies. His parents taught him not to believe El Diablo.

Send La Muerte! someone shouted.

No, Vendo said. The old hag likes Randy. See how tenderly she holds his Roots of Life.

Send Mabelline!

Oh, no. She's past her prime. Did you see how terrible she looks? The boys don whistle anymore.

Take him to Todospedo! Let the mayor punish him!

Yes! the mob shouted. Todospedo will judge!

Dragging their withered bodies, the mob raised a cloud of dust that covered the sun. The stench that rose was poisonous.

They found Todospedo at the potato vodka booth. Drunk as a skunk and smelling decomposed.

When Compro and Vendo explained what was happening, Todospedo rose up like a demon in a whirlwind.

Why wern I tol this? Burp. I wun low a bridge! Burp. I neber haf! Burp. We don wanna know whas on dat side! Legends say ees full uv dead poets! Din we outlaw poets? Burp.

Yes! Compro said. We must stop em! Building a bridge is madness!

Poetry is madness! Vendo shouted.

Sofia of the Lambs lives there, the innocent child said, but she was drowned out by the mob.

What do we do? asked Vendo.

Grab the sucker! Bring im to me! Todospedo commanded. He mus have a weakness. Burp. Evry man has a tragic flaw, as the Geeks said. Whas *his* weakness?

He wants to be remembered, Compro whispered.

What?

He keeps asking if anyone remembers him.

He wans to be remembered! Todospedo thundered. Thas it! Thas his flaw! Don he know only those in histry books are remembered?

N history is full of fairy tales! Vendo added. Fantasies for those who wanna be remembered. What egos! What arrogance!

Hasn he learned tha *here* is without hope? We never thought bout a bridge! We don wanna bridge!

We don wanna bridge! The mob took up the refrain. The sun grew dark. The birds and the animals fled. A rain of scavenging locusts fell upon the pomegranate tree.

But history also teaches us lessons! the innocent child cried.

Todospedo shouted her down. What do *you* know? Go back where you came from! A closet poet! Or worse!

The child moved away, like a cloud without a home.

Now I know Randy's tragic fault! Todospedo said. I will beguile him.

How? Vendo asked.

Simple. I'll tell im he can leave Agua Bendita n return to time-past.

Time-past, the mob shuddered. The word drove fear into their dry hearts, painful as the nails driven into Christ's hands. All souls present had dreamed of returning to *time-past*. But no one ever had. And no one dared to mention such a thought.

There were no maps, no directions. No one had ever looked back. Legend said the two-headed calf would turn those who looked back into pillars of salt. Or worse— they would become lost souls who could never return to their ancestral land.

He caint refuse! Bring im to me!

The mob waited for Randy by the side of the road. The Road of Life. When Randy came whistling by with Oso at his heels, the mob grabbed him and took him before Todospedo.

Crafty Todospedo greeted Randy like a long-lost son. Come sit by me, he said, vodka spittle wetting his tangled beard. We ave to talk. So many things to discuss.

A puzzled Randy asked, Do you know me?

Course I do. You're Randy Lopez. A teacher gave you that name cause she couldn pronounce the names of the three saints. I know your parents, the house with the pomegranate tree. Such kind people.

Yes! Randy cried. Glory to God! Someone finally remembers me! Tears filled his eyes.

He flung his arms around Todospedo.

I do belong! I do belong! he shouted. My life among the gringos has not been for naught!

Naught was the kind of word his writing teacher had told him he should use every once in a while. For effect. Old English still impressed people.

Randy took Todospedo's cold, dry hands. How can I thank you for remembering me?

No need, Todospedo replied. It's my job as mayor to make sure things run smoothly in Agua Bendita. So I'm gonna make you an offer you caint refuse.

An offer? Randy looked at the mob. All were smiling. Did they trust Todospedo? Should he?

How'd you like to return to time-past? Thas the offer. If you agree to go away, you can return to your past life. Then it'll all be as it was in Agua Bendita fore you came.

Randy couldn't believe what he had heard.

What? Return?

Yes, Todospedo replied. You can go back. Forget the bridge. Forget Sofia of the Lambs. Forget what you've seen or tasted here. You can go back.

Oh, Lord! Randy cried. Is it possible?

Of course, Todospedo said, placing his arm sweetly around Randy.

Randy grew cautious. He knew the Devil used many disguises and he loved to make offers. Hadn't he tempted Jesus on the mountain?

But I thought no one could return.

It can be done! Todospedo insisted.

By whose authority? Randy asked. He wasn't taking chances.

By my authority! Todospedo exclaimed. And everyone here agrees. The elders give their word. Say yes and you return to time-past. This is my final offer!

Twenty

The Devil waves a wand and Randy sees images of people he knew in *time-past*. Randy is tempted to return.

Imagine a man shipwrecked on an island so lost in the time of legends his story seems the stuff of fantasy. Such a man is Ulysseus. Seven years ago he crashed his ship into the island of Calypso the sea nymph.

She is one of the most beautiful nymphs in the Aegean world. She provides Ulysseus with everything he desires. Pleasures beyond description, a harem to do his bidding, and a stupendous seaside mansion. If he stays with her, she promises him immortality.

What more could a man want?

Still, every afternoon Ulysseus sits on the beach and dreams of home. In the flaming clouds of the setting sun he sees his wife Penelope. Virtuous at her loom. He sees his son, who has grown into young manhood. He envisions his fields of wheat, his olive trees, his horses, and his oxen.

He dreams of time-past. Disquietude fills his soul.

Seven years adds up to a season in the esoteric gospels. Time of renewal.

A love-prisoner cared for by Calypso, and he is not happy.

The nymph notes it has affected their sex life.

A man dreaming of things as they used to be in time-past is not a happy camper. Memoria haunts his sleeping and waking.

Memoria is a constant guest. She can create the most pleasant fantasies or she can be muy cabrona. When she stirs the soul, !ni modo! Images flood the mind's eye! Wild as untamed horses! No one can control the images of Memoria. Poets have tried. Bullshit!

When least expected, she tosses memories at you like a sailor tossing coins on the bar. Drinks for everyone! I've been at sea too long!

Memories you thought you had forgotten appear. Shades of Señor Freud!

The images she offers can make your day or wreck your life. She is drunk with power!

Whence the images? we ask. Are they caused by the cheese we ate at dinner? Undigested, it can cause gas and crazy thoughts. Or are such memories archetypal? You know, Jungian. Good luck guessing, tonto.

Memoria doesn't care. Dreams are my sisters, she croons. Sueños. Near-death experiences. Daydreams. My dream-images are why some become saints and others go insane.

She laughs at those who would control her.

Still, without memory we would not be human. Take it or leave it. Better take it, pendejo.

But you have everything here in Ogygia! Calypso reminds Ulysseus. My island is magical.

Yes, but I miss the way it used to be.

Used to be! she shouts. Nothing is as it used to be! Penelope has grown old; your son will not recognize you. The horses you loved and trained are long-dead and have become food for the worms. The suitors have eaten your stores of grain and cattle, drunk your wine!

I know, Ulysseus whispers, but there must be something I can recapture there. If only I could embrace my wife again, taste her lips, smell her body's perfume. I want to show my son how to string my bow, behold the flowering of my olive trees, walk in the pleasing horse-smell of my stables, hear the sea slopping against my shore. If only! he cries to the Olympian gods.

My! My! My! Calypso shouts. Men! Okay, go!

She relents and grants him permission to leave. Poseidon will destroy you, she warns him. You will never see Ithaca, your homeland. Your wife has cut down your marriage bed and used it for firewood. Your son will drive you away. Not even Argos your arthritic dog will know you. Everything is against you. Go if you wish!

A nymph spurned is a nymph wasted. Still Ulysseus kisses her goodbye and sets off on his raft, his odyssey begun.

So it is with Randy. He's no Ulysseus to be sure, but he, too, has been given a chance to return.

Todospedo and the mob await his answer.

Three times he asks Todospedo if the offer is sincere, and three times the mayor swears on Sofia's honor that the offer is cast in gold.

Time-past, Randy whispered, and licked his lips. Time as it used to be.

He had not thought of his prior life till now. He has been too busy with the exigencies of Agua Bendita. Now the images of time-past flood his senses.

Will I have space to move around?

You can have all the space-time you need. That's the deal.

What will I do if I take the offer?

Do what you want, Todospedo replied.

I would read more books. Yes! I would live in a library and read everything.

Miss Libriana beamed with pride. What a noble soul resides in her second son.

———

I would study! Learn the cultures of the world. Learn languages!

Father Polonio scowled. I knew it! He wants to learn Hebrew. True son of Levi that he is!

I would fill my home not just with country western and mariachi music, I would listen to classical music from all over the world. Music from China, the Congo, Nepal, Muslim calls to prayer— my Freddy Fender and Johnny Cash CDs!

I like that, his friend Pedro Peñasco said. Wish I could travel with you, hermano. We would sail the seven seas on a sturdy galleon. What a brave new world that would be. But it's not possible, he said in a voice so forlorn the sound made the great owls of the forest cry. No, I cannot go. The offer is only for you. My work is here.

Pedro, you have to save souls drowning in the River of Life.

Así es, Pedro replied.

What else? Todospedo asked impatiently.

I would like to marry and have children, Randy whispered.

Mabelline let out a heart-wrenching cry. She loved Randy but realized she could not return with him to time-past. Her sobs were like the cries of mourning doves at the end of day.

Go on, Todospedo said.

I want to play baseball again. Like we did when we were kids. In the nettle-infested dusty field catching fly balls, running and sweating, later a dip in the cool river. I loved my childhood friends. I would give anything to see them again.

He paused. His throat constricted with emotion when he thought of his parents. He had hesitated mentioning them because he knew he would cry.

The memory of his parents was more than he could bear. Covering his face with both hands, he let out an anguished plea.

!Mis viejitos! !Ay, mis viejitos! !Cómo los amo! !Quiero estar con ustedes otra vez!

His warm tears flowed from a depth of soul so deep that even the mob was moved to crying. On the hill the mocking-birds warbled a melody usually reserved for funerals.

What hero has not cried when he remembers mother and father, remembers friends living in the mist of time-past? Ulysseus shed anguished tears in Hades, and Jesus wept in hell for lost souls. Tears of remembrance are tears of redemption.

!Papá! !Mamá! Randy shouted. I want to be with you! To touch your lovely faces. I want to live in the circle of your love again. Oh how sweet was life in our simple home. I need your blessing again. I need those special moments we shared so long ago.

It can all be yours again! Todospedo tempted. He motioned and the Devil and La Muerte stepped forward.

Show Randy what he can have! Show im things as they used to be! Let im see the images of time-past! Let im smell damp earth after a rain! Stand in the presence of a brilliant sunset! Enjoy his friends! His favorite foods!

Show im his parents!

The Devil waved a withered hand, and the images of Randy's parents appeared.

Randy reached for them.

!Mamá! !Papá! He fell to his knees crying.

Don't be stupid, the Devil whispered. Take his offer! The minute you say yes you can be with them. !Anda! Time's a'wasting!

It can be as it used to be, La Muerte said. She held up Randy's bleeding Roots of Life, ganglion still squirming with a bit of life. The roots that once connected him to earth.

Randy heard the far-away scream of an ambulance racing toward the wrecked train outside Santa Fe. He picked up Oso and held the small dog to his chest.

I can't! he cried. My roots are severed!

No problem, La Muerte said. With my spittle I weave them together. Life returns!

She spat in one hand, like a shortstop spitting into his glove, ready to catch the line drive that would end the inning.

La Muerte rubbed the spittle, the juice of life, into the roots she held. They squirmed with life.

!Ne seas pendejo! the Devil coaxed. Take the deal!

For a moment Randy believed his roots could be attached again to the earth he once knew.

Was La Muerte the third Fate, dull scissors in hand? She who cut the roots. There was no mention of a fourth Fate in the ancient histories. No promise of resurrection.

Here are your parents, the Devil pointed. Waiting for you. All you have to do is look back!

A trembling Randy reached for his father and mother. He grasped the air, crying !Mamá! !Papá!

His cries cracked the hearts of those present. The women wept. The mob protested. Enough! Enough! Let him go! Why torture the man?

The chorus spoke, but Todospedo would not listen.

Everything you desire can be yours! he shouted. You wanna be with your parents. You can taste your mother's cooking. In the afternoons you and your father tossed a football— remember his laughter and strong arms!

Yes! Randy cried. Oh, to be in his arms again!

Remember your friends from time-past! The neighborhood where you lived, coffee in the morning, sunshine on the apple trees, your mother's geraniums, the phases of the moon, the girl who lived next door, the night you kissed her, the fragrance of her body—

Stop! Randy cried. All men yearn to return! I will spit out the pomegranate seed stuck between my teeth and look back! I will look back!

The mob fell silent as doom.

This was the last temptation of Randy Lopez.

He was ready to accept the offer.

My son, my son, crooned Todospedo, holding forth a contract for Randy to sign.

Sign on the dotted line and it shall be. You will return to *time-past*. One of the few men in recorded history to do so. You will be received as a hero in that world of illusions.

Yes! Todospedo shouted, turning to the mob. Randy Lopez will be called a hero. His name will be immortal. He will have many stories to tell his grandchildren. How he came to the country of Agua Bendita and learned *there* is *here*!

He turned to Randy. Sign here, he whispered, offering the charred paper that burned with a sulfurous fire such as only angels possess.

The pen Randy took also sprouted fire.

The hushed mob sighed in unison. Randy Lopez was going home.

Twenty-one

Building a bridge is dangerous work, but Sofia is constant. She waits for those who seek her.

How does it feel to be here? Eliseo asked.

Randy looked at the mexicano workers, who had gathered around him.

I feel like a new man, he answered.

Was making the decision difficult?

Yes. I thought of my past life and everything I wanted to do there. But in my heart of hearts I know I belong here.

That was an awesome offer, Eliseo said. No one else has ever been in that situation. Maybe Dante and those guys who visited hell. They came back. But those are only stories in books.

Books are alive with truth, Randy said. We all live our stories. Time-past was one story. Now my purpose is here.

The bridge? Eliseo asked.

That and other things, Randy replied.

Did you look back?

I saw images of those I left behind. There was beauty and love in that world. But there is beauty and love here.

You're brave, Eliseo said. He was proud of his childhood friend.

Not brave, Randy replied. *Here* is where I belong.

The workers nodded. He had been tempted and had resisted. They respected him for that.

Unica spoke. The young want to know why you didn't take Todospedo's offer.

Randy answered, I already lived my life in time-past. Now my work is here. I understand now that crossing from there to here is part of the natural cycles you describe so well. Todospedo's offer was the Devil's temptation. His lie would disrupt the laws of nature. I accepted the natural path. My time now is here.

Amen, Unica said. You have learned the greatest lesson. But the young are tempted daily. Where do they find the strength to resist?

We must teach them the natural laws, Randy replied. As you teach us. If a fellow human is in need, we must help. The circle of family and community is stronger than isolation.

Así es, Unica said. Goodness flows when we help each other. Soul and body are entwined like two strands of a DNA molecule. Essence and flesh flow from nature. And they return to nature. The soul returns to Tata Dios. The Great Mystery of the universe goes on spinning. There is no beginning and no end. This is the lesson of Agua Bendita.

Así es, the workers whispered.

Oso barked, Asssi-es! and ran to play with the children.

Are you sure of your decision? Unica asked.

Sure as the sun shines, Randy said.

He looked across the river. Sofia and her lambs waited on the opposite bank. She waved. Randy waved back. He could see her clearly. Her face shone with the beauty of one who carries truth in her heart. She had waited for him all those years, and he yearned to be with her.

The bridge was almost complete. The mexicano workers had figured out how to place the huge timbers and lay the planks. After all, in time-past their ancestors had constructed magnificent cities and pyramids.

The workers had been joined by many from the village. The

young especially had taken the challenge. They worked at sawing planks, smoothing them, and hauling them down the mountain.

They sang as they worked. The singing pines and the melody of the river joined in, adding the final stanzas to the new corrido. *We came to work. . . . ¡Aquí estamos y no nos vamos!*

But a question still hung in the air.

Where is one's true home?

The universe is my home, Randy answered. I am made of stardust. Mother earth is my home. I am of the clay people. On this most incredible planet, Agua Bendita is my home. Where there is home, there is work to do.

He pointed at the bridge.

A beautiful bridge, María said.

The bridge shone like the rainbows angels weave with sunlight after a rain. Far more enchanting than the imaginary bridge the Devil had described.

El puente del Diablo es ilusión, José said. The Devil's bridge is an illusion. This bridge is real. We made it with our manos. Ahora we go to el norte. ¡Este es el Puente de la Vida!

¡El Puente de la Vida! the workers cheered. The Bridge of Life!

Sí. Puente de la Vida. Future workers will know its name. And they will know the name Randy Lopez.

¡Viva Randy! the workers shouted. Their cry echoed to the farthest corner of Agua Bendita, rousing those who thought they were dead.

Finally a bridge they could use. No more drownings in treacherous rivers. Bridges could be built across the River of Life.

Randy's godparents came to stand near him.

You have given us a purpose, his padrino said. He hugged

Randy. So what if they gave you a gringo name? Now many of our children have gringo names. !Que vivan los gringos!

The workers answered, !Viva Mexico! !Vivan los gringos! They tossed their hats in the air.

You turned out to be a good boy, Randy's madrina said. She handed Randy his baptismal certificate, where the names of the three saints were revealed.

Randy read the certificate and smiled. The names were a blessing on his head.

Gracias, Madrina.

Your ancestors watch over you, Padrino said. They are the santitos who guide you. Tu mamá y papá y los abuelos. They taught you to be kind and do good deeds. We honor them.

!Así es! the workers cheered. !Vivan los santitos!

The cry echoed across the river.

Miss Libriana beamed. Her cheeks sported a lively color. She was eager to haul books across the river. There she would find readers. Already the young had begun to read during rest periods. The knowledge of the world was coming alive again.

Father Polonio nodded approval. He planned to look for souls in need of the sacraments on the other side. And he promised the conversos he would bless their Friday prayers. He and the children of Levi Rael had become working buddies. Live and let live, the priest said. Although he still ribbed them about not eating pork.

Pedro de Peñasco had taken back the name of the village of his birth. Already he had fished out two workers who had fallen into the river. Building bridges can be dangerous work, as anyone who ever built one can testify. But with Pedro at the ready, no one had drowned or been hurt.

The bridge had been blessed by Sofia.

My father's fields lie fallow, Randy said. They are overgrown with nettles. We will plow the weeds under and dig out the acequia. We will plant corn, squash, chile verde, tomatoes. Lilith is an expert gardener. She can teach us. Soon we will have vegetables to cook with the potatoes.

I can learn to cook! Mabelline exclaimed in a burst of passion. The young men nearby sighed and closed their poetry books. Mabelline in the kitchen conjured up a flow of erotic images like those described in the Cama Sultry.

I will water the pomegranate tree and it will flower again, Abel's Daughter said. Imagine pomegranate juice for the tired spirits of Agua Bendita. Renewal.

The workers cheered her. Pomegranate juice had not been served in Agua Bendita since the time of legends.

I can teach the way of Zen, the Zen master said. And teach dance to the children.

Angelica sang a sweet melody. My children will play with the lambs. They will be safe from beasts of terror.

In the cantina Squat turned to Bob. Those mejicanos sure did a fine job.

Meh-jee-ka-nos? Bob mangled the word. Whered ju learn that muey correct-toe Spanish?

They're here to stay. Might as well be neighbors. I wan my grankids to talk to em, not fear em. Come on, let's join em.

Bob looked around the cantina. Beats this here place. Vamoose.

Vamos, Squat corrected. They went out laughing.

So much to do, Randy said. I want to repair my father's house. Plant grass and trees in the cemetery. Instead of the Dance of the Dead we will have the Dance of Life. A fiesta of life.

!Viva la Fiesta de la Vida! the workers cheered.

So much to do.

It *is* a time of transformation, Unica said.

As I was taught by you. By all of you.

Finally there was some joy in Agua Bendita.

Back to work! José called. In a few hours we finish. Then we cross!

Oso barked. He had become the playmate of the children and loved every moment.

The Devil turned to La Muerte. Looks like we're not needed here, comadre. Vámonos.

Ungrateful dead, La Muerte said. Así es. Vamos.

Arm in arm, they turned away, perhaps to find other places in which to converse and strategize. She to cut the Roots of Life, he to tempt with lies.

Sofia's cherry tree is ripe with dark, sweet cherries, Unica said to Randy. It's a good day to cross to the shore where wisdom reigns.

What of the legend? Randy asked. It has been said that thrice she lost her virginity and regained it.

Wisdom has lost her virginity many times, Unica explained. She suffered much during the three world wars. Those times people forgot their innate wisdom, and the world went up in flames. Fear turned nation against nation. Friend against friend.

Three world wars, Randy mused. What a waste.

Yes. And it's not just war. Every day Sofia is assaulted by prejudices, stupidity, deceit, the powerful abusing the weak, the plight of poor women. Those blows weaken her, but she springs anew in the heart of the just.

She has been my constant love for a long time, Randy said. I made a vow to protect her. The young who cross with us will learn to honor her.

Sofia loves the young, Unica agreed. They are her spring

lambs. With wisdom in their hearts, they become lovers of beauty and truth. People will remember Agua Bendita. Your decision to stay was not just for you, it was also for them.

They looked at the throng of workers ready to cross the river. Their numbers spread to infinity.

So many need the bridge, Randy said. What a glorious time. I truly feel I am home.

He waved at Sofia and she waved back.

Be still my heart, he whispered. Soon.

Twenty-two

Randy learns a bridge is never completely finished. It requires constant attention and repair.

Randy looked back.

This surprised Unica.

You looked back?

Yes.

What did you see?

Spirits coming up the canyon. Stumbling in the dark, seeking their dreams. They will pass by Todos Santos and the two-headed calf and think they are lost. They must know there is a bridge here so they do not lose hope.

Unica smiled. The young man who rode up the dark canyon on a sway-back mare had grown in wisdom. He built a bridge for the people of Agua Bendita and those to come.

I love him like a son, she thought. I made a vow never to love again, and I love Randy Lopez.

You're crying, Randy said.

Not me, kid, Unica replied, rubbing her eyes. I got dust in my eyes. That's all.

Randy smiled and looked at the ground, where a few ants had begun to venture out. In the air were barely visible flying specks. Tiny fruit flies. Insects emerging from their eggs and shells. The dry shells throbbed with life.

Unica pointed.

A horned moon rose over the eastern shoulder of the mountain. Bright enough to light the way for la Virgen de Guadalupe. Or the Buddha. The Star of Bethlehem also shone brightly. Enough light for all prophets. The heavens were offering a blessing.

A new season, Randy whispered.

Así es, Unica whispered. Across the river the sun shines for Sofia. Warmth for the lambs.

Even here?

Yes, even here. ?Por qué no? Maybe there is more renewal here than in time-past. We take what we get.

Así es, Randy agreed, and turned to greet his parents, who came hurrying to his side.

!Mamá! !Papá!

He hugged his mother and father and the love he felt sent the cold clouds scuttling away. Sun, moon, and stars were returning to Agua Bendita.

I went for seeds I had saved, his father said, holding up a bag. Pomegranate, apple, corn, chile, pumpkin, zucchini. For the other side. We will farm as we used to.

I washed your jacket, his mother said, handing him the clean jacket. I don't want you to get cold.

Still taking care of me. I could not ask for more loving parents.

Ay, hijo, they said proudly. We waited for you. Now we are united. Is it time to cross?

Yes, Randy replied.

The workers finished putting in place the last span of the bridge. Excitement bristled in the air.

Those who doubted a bridge to wisdom could ever be built turned away. Naysayers. They left a trail of rust and dust.

Your dream, Unica said.

Is it real? Randy whispered.

As real as corn on the cob, she answered.

The workers laughed. Elotes cocidos. Con mantequilla. Their mouths watered. They were tired of potatoes. Over there they would grow many vegetables. Cuatro Milpas would flower again. The weak complexions of the children would improve. Life would improve.

Es real, Randy! José exclaimed, slapping Randy on the back. Thank you, hermano!

Are you sure it's safe? Randy asked. He worried for them. He worried for the children.

Es safe, José assured him. We cross muchos deserts and rivers. Many amigos y amigas die. Now we have the bridge. Mira, amigo, we know a puente always needs work. Every year we come and make it more strong. Como se dice— repair. Así es la vida.

A wise man, Unica said.

Randy agreed. He had learned that transformations are never done. They go on spinning. That was the lesson of Agua Bendita. The essence and the flesh just go on becoming. Trees become bridges. The universe spins toward new beginnings. Nothing is lost.

The process of becoming requires constant repair, Unica said. Rome wasn't built in a day.

Randy nodded. He turned to José. Where will you go?

To el norte to work. My compañeros are strong. We work hard. Denver, Chicago, many place. We help build this country. Es our country now. Some want to go to East L.A. The chamacos go to college there.

The young nodded. A new country. Dreams of school. Many Chicanos and Chicanas had already entered professions. Some were teachers. They would help.

!Sí, se puede! the young shouted. We will live and work with the americanos.

Randy smiled. He appreciated their courage. But he worried.

Many things will change, he said. You have to learn English, customs, history, movies, music, so much.

We can do it! they cried.

The young could do it, but what of José y María? Randy turned to José. La cultura de los americanos es muy diferente.

Es okay, Randy. We learn. Our familias are strong.

The workers agreed. Yes, we can!

The cultures of el norte and those of the south were different. Would the americanos give the mexicanos time to adjust? Would the cultures blend? Learn to live side by side? No doubt the time of adjustment would be painful. Or would the americanos insist the way of the gringo was the only way?

We understand, María said. Mucho cambia. But for our children, we go. Que venga lo que venga.

Randy smiled. They were strong women. For their children they would tackle the future. Come what may.

Change is constant, Unica said. The world is changing. Even Agua Bendita changed. There is hope.

José took off his cap and wiped the sweat from his forehead. We do it, Randy. Like my wife say. !Que venga lo que venga!

We work hard, María added. We make this country our country. They be proud of us.

We take a new flag, José said. The workers agreed. A new bandera. Red, white, and blue.

But we don forget our patria. We don forget our ancestors. Everything can be together en el corazón.

Así es, Randy said.

María smiled and put her arm around her husband. Estamos listos. Randy, you cross first. They wait for you.

The workers had gathered their tools and belongings and were ready to cross. They turned to him. He should lead them.

Ran-deee! they shouted. Come! You first, amigo!

Es your bridge, José said proudly.

No, amigo, Randy replied, placing his hand on his friend's shoulder. The bridge belongs to all of us. It belongs to the community for all to use. We will cross together.

Unica touched his arm. Look.

Oso was not waiting. He had seen Sofia's children across the river. He barked and raced across the bridge and onto land.

Faloooo me! he barked and ran happily into Sofia's arms. He ran to play with the lambs, Sofia's children.

The workers cheered.

!Vamos! Randy called. It's time!

He made sure mothers with children and old people crossed first. He helped his parents and his padrino and madrina.

Singing their new corrido, the workers marched across. The bridge welcomed the stamping feet. A new land opened her arms to receive them.

Sofia ran to embrace Randy and a heavenly perfume of love filled the air. Kind of like just-popped popcorn at the movie house. Or like when your mom baked tortillas on the stove and the kitchen was filled with the most satisfying aroma in the world.

Welcome home, my love. I have waited for you.

Her touch filled Randy's heart with beauty and truth. Love and inner wisdom filled his soul.

Gracias, he whispered. I yearned for this moment for so long.

Come, she said. The journey begins. New adventures.

At that moment Randy understood what Unica had taught: The soul goes on spinning. There is no beginning; there is no end. Nothing is lost.

Sofia took his hand and they walked across the sweetgrass meadow into a shining new dream.

Oso barked and followed. The children and the workers followed.

New horizons opened before them. Brand new worlds all waiting to be explored.

The journey begins

A Note to the Reader:
How Randy Lopez Came to Me

My wife, Patricia, died in January 2010. During her illness, we cared for her at home and were privileged to be part of the transformation she went through. Pain and the dissolution of her body were involved, but also, as one of our daughters said, "She grew lovelier and more ethereal."

The first month of her illness, I had a vision. Perhaps I should say the vision came to me, unexpectedly. The images of the first chapter of *Randy Lopez Goes Home* appeared, clear and forceful. I saw Randy ride the sway-back mare into the village, stop for the tarantula, and meet the two old men at the cantina. I instantly knew the young man was Randy Lopez. The cast of characters Randy would meet in Agua Bendita also came without effort.

"I don't know where these characters are coming from," I said to Patricia.

"They need you to write their story," she answered. She knew the workings of my imagination.

When I finished a chapter, I hurried to share it with her. She was always intensely interested in my work. I am grateful she was able to read the entire first draft. When she was done reading she put the manuscript on her lap and smiled. "You have something important here," she said.

Because of her, I began to believe in Randy Lopez.

I continued working on the story. Patricia's energy was diminishing; she could no longer read. Each day we sat together and I described how the story was growing. One day she said the most telling thing anyone could ever say about the novel. She said with all the wisdom and understanding that shone in her clear blue eyes: "I feel Randy Lopez is a long-lost lover."

I looked at her with wonder. She understood and accepted the transformations she and Randy were going through. Of course Randy was her lover. She was dying, as Randy dies in the story. She knew I was searching for some truth or faith to sustain us during her passage. Randy's journey was a healing process for us, an acceptance of what was coming. Randy had found a purpose in the hereafter. I had found a purpose in writing his story. I had honored the vision. We would both be stronger as we faced Patricia's last days on earth.

Characters have always appeared to me and asked me to write their stories. I thank the spirit of Randy Lopez for coming to me. I, too, learned to love him. I hope this allegorical story helps others renew their faith in the transformative powers of the soul. It did for me and Patricia. During her hospice period, our love grew stronger than ever. Difficult? Yes. Letting go of one's soul mate is not easy.

I have faith in the healing powers of the soul. The soul *is* the creative imagination, and it keeps leading us into profound depths that each one of us must explore. Those explorations are the soul's journey, the journey of our humanity.

I am now writing a series of stories in which the grieving soul communicates with the departed soul. Each day brings new revelations— the essence is rich with limitless illuminations. I know that in time I will meet Patricia in the spirit world, that vast world we know so little about. Sharing our stories provides windows into that universe. We know that nothing is lost of the flesh or of the spirit. That is the lesson of Randy's odyssey, the message from Agua Bendita, the strength and faith Patricia gave us. We learned we must renew our purpose daily.

We must bless all of life.

Also by Rudolfo Anaya

Bless Me, Ultima
Heart of Aztlan
Tortuga
The Silence of the Llano
The Legend of La Llorona
The Adventures of Juan Chicaspatas
A Chicano in China
Lord of the Dawn: The Legend of Quetzalcóatl
Alburquerque
The Anaya Reader
Zia Summer
Jalamanta: A Message from the Desert
Rio Grande Fall
Shaman Winter
Serafina's Stories
Jemez Spring
Curse of the ChupaCabra
The Man Who Could Fly and Other Stories
ChupaCabra and the Roswell UFO
The Essays

Children's Books

The Farolitos of Christmas: A New Mexico Christmas Story
Farolitos for Abuelo
My Land Sings: Stories from the Rio Grande
Elegy on the Death of César Chávez
Roadrunner's Dance
The Santero's Miracle: A Bilingual Story
The First Tortilla: A Bilingual Story
Juan and the Jackalope: A Children's Book in Verse